se

TRAPPED IN DARKNESS, FIGHTING FOR SURVIVAL, THEIR ONLY WEAPON IS LOVE.

SAFE NOW

TAYLOR ANNE VIGIL

Table of Contents

Safe Now

Trigger Warning

THIS BOOK CONTAINS scenes of intense physical violence, including graphic descriptions of beatings, injuries, and fight scenes. It also features depictions of kidnapping, captivity, and psychological trauma, such as panic attacks and severe anxiety. The story involves threats of sexual violence and other forms of abuse. Discussions and depictions of self-harm, suicidal ideation, and attempts are present. Additionally, there are elements of emotional manipulation and trauma related to relationships. Readers sensitive to these topics should proceed with caution.

Content Warning

THIS BOOK INCLUDES the following potentially distressing content:

- Physical violence and fight scenes
- Kidnapping and captivity
- Psychological trauma, including panic attacks and severe anxiety
- Threats of sexual violence
- Graphic descriptions of injuries and medical distress
- Discussions and depictions of self-harm, suicidal ideation, and attempts
- Emotional manipulation and trauma related to relationships
- Graphic depictions of blood and injuries
- Scenes of intense emotional distress and crying

Readers who may be affected by these themes should be aware and take care while reading.

Dedication

To my brothers: Thank you for enriching my childhood. This book was written for you.

Prologue

Avan winced, shuffling to make room for me on the hospital bed. I laced my fingers with his, careful of his IV, and laid my head against the pillow.

"Promise me," I whispered, fighting back tears. "This one was your last."

He lifted our tangled fingers to his lips and kissed them.

"I promise," he said.

With another wince, he rolled onto his side and touched my cheek. I echoed his actions, stroking my fingers through his hair. For a while we stayed like that, softly touching, our lips inches apart, staring into one another's eyes. His breath warmed my skin as he murmured to me.

"I promise you. No more fighting. You're more important."

He forced a smile and, for his sake, I smiled back. Then my chest tightened and I couldn't breathe. Images of him, my sweet Avan, going down, hitting his head, lying motionless, replayed over and over in my head. I remembered the sound the most, the sickening *"Whack! Whack!"* of the opponent's foot striking is face. I shivered and fought for air.

"Hey," Avan soothed, resting his palms on either side of my neck. "I'm okay. Look at me. It's okay."

Then, just as he'd done so many times before, he breathed with me. He shushed me and he breathed, inhaling deeply through his nose and exhaling through his mouth, despite how much it irritated the nagging injuries to his chest. I breathed with him. I focused on the sound of my heartbeat, the softness of his hands, his lips on my forehead. Slowly I calmed, catching my breath and burying my face into the warm skin of his neck.

"I don't want to watch you get hurt anymore," I whimpered through trembling breaths. "I can't."

He shushed me again and pressed his lips against my ear. I heard his breathing grow uneven as he pulled me closer.

"You won't have to."

Chapter One

I clutched the steering wheel as the tires struggled to grip the slick road. I could see nothing but the headlights shining feebly off the random patches of ice. Cold trailed up my back.

The warmth of Avan's hand brought me back to calmness. He was always warm.

I glanced over. He smiled and took my hand from the steering wheel, cradling it in both of his, his fingers fiddling with mine.

"I can drive," he offered.

His touch was like his voice, loving and soft. I smiled back at him. He chuckled, reading my answer in my raised eyebrow.

I couldn't wait to get the cabin. I couldn't wait to breathe in the sharp scent of the wintergreens surrounding it and see the clear lake. I couldn't wait to sit by the fireplace and eat marshmallows after a romantic candlelight dinner. I couldn't wait to get away from the fumes of the city and soak up a relaxing, rustic weekend with Avan.

At that moment, I could see the rest of my life stretched out in front of me. I saw it so perfectly: Avan and I nestled in a cozy little cottage, our children running and playing in the snow, our dogs playing with them.

Despite my dreams, despite my hopes, a feeling of uneasiness crept over me again and stayed. Avan leaned in and kissed below my ear, but even that couldn't dispel the feeling of lurking dread. I glimpsed the twinkle of the lake out of the corner of my eye, but the feeling never left. It was an eerie feeling like, like-

The Bronco jerked. My window shattered. We rolled. There was a huge splash, and thousands of knives cut into my skin as icy water rushed through the broken window into the car. I reached into the water, fumbling at my seat belt, my hands numb.

Avan gasped for breath beside me as water rose over my head. We were sinking, drowning, dying. My lungs burned. There was just enough light for me to see Avan struggling to unbuckle his own seat belt, then hit the window with his elbow, but then I turned to my problems. My heart pounded, my lungs screaming for air. I was suffocating.

Avan's hands came into view, reaching down and grabbing my belt buckle. I felt the seat belt loosen and helped tug it out of the way. Avan pushed me toward the shattered window, urging me to swim through the shark-looking gap. Shards of glass snagged my jacket and shirt, holding me back. I struggled frantically, panic setting in, glass slicing into my fingertips as I clawed for escape.

Someone grabbed my hand, pulling me up, away from the car, closer to the surface. I broke through into the cold air, gasping and coughing, my legs too weak to support me, too tired to move. Someone else wrapped their arms around me and dragged me to the shore. Hands dug into my coat pockets the second I was dropped onto the snow. Something was tossed into the water. I shivered, too numb to feel, to care about anything other than the next breath. In the dull light of the moon, I saw the silhouette of a man, kneeling over me, his movements frantic.

Was it Avan?

No. I'd left Avan behind, in the water, in the cold.

There was a tiny pinch in the crook of my arm, and a thick blanket was laid on top of me. I knew I was safe. Dimly I remembered Avan, abandoned, under the water, but it seemed too difficult to say anything, let alone move.

I was lifted and carried to a rumbling truck. The man laid me in the back, on top of more blankets. With painful tingles I felt the feeling in my fingers returning. A rough sensation embraced my wrists, tightening as the man hovered over me.

Something was wrong.

As the nerves in the rest of my body regained sensation, I realized I had the same tight feeling around my ankles too. I couldn't move.

A male voice shouted over me, from what I thought might be the driver's seat. "Where the Hell is he?"

Someone burst out of the water. Over the rumbling of the truck engine I heard the sound of swimming, then dragging, the crunching and displacement of snow.

Avan was out of the water! It *had* to be him.

I tried to move, but couldn't. I was floating, relaxing as if I was in a warm pool. Something was pulling me under. My thoughts fogged and drifted. My eyes were suddenly heavy, and my vision blurred and darkened.

Another voice, a different man, shouted from afar. "He's not breathing!"

The rougher voice called back, menacing, angry. "Then make him breathe!"

No, it couldn't be Avan they talked about, could it? He had to have gotten out of the car. He *had* to! I strained, listening. To my immense relief, Avan coughed violently, then gasped.

"GET AWAY FROM HER!"

My eyes fluttered open at the sound of Avan's furious bellow. Wait. If he was yelling, then it wasn't Avan who was on top of me! I focused, my eyes fighting my mind's commands, and saw a balding man, a stranger with black eyes and a scarred face. I was lying on a bed, my wrists tied to the posts. The stranger gripped my neck with calloused fingers. A small, pathetic whimper rose from my throat. Instinct told me to struggle, to kick, to scream, but I couldn't.

"Don't touch her!" Avan roared. He grunted and cursed. I still couldn't see him, but I knew he was struggling against bonds like mine.

The stranger looked over his shoulder, hand still on my neck. "Or what?"

Avan's voice became even, his tone deep and menacing. "Or I'll fucking kill you."

The stranger erupted in a burst of laughter but eased his grip. I held my breath. I closed my eyes and prepared myself for whatever this stranger wanted to do to me. He climbed off the bed, off me, and headed for Avan.

I inhaled sharply and fought to sit up, managing enough to see, and what I saw froze me in place. Avan's wrists were secured to a support beam, his arms high above his head, the beam low enough for his toes to touch the ground. He wasn't wearing the jacket or long-sleeved shirt he'd left home in. A thin muscle shirt was all he had above the black sweatpants he wore this morning. His feet were bare, his wool socks and scuffed boots nowhere in sight. In the background, an air conditioner hummed.

Our captor circled him now in a way that made my stomach churn. "Avan Gutierrez," he said, sounding giddy. "What a gifted fighter you were, huh?"

The stranger ambled around him, utterly confident, scanning Avan up and down, and I examined him in turn. He looked like he could lift a truck. In comparison, Avan was thin, lanky, and not the least bit threatening-looking, but I'd seen him fight. I watched him knock countless opponents to their knees with one swift kick to the ribs. I watched him stand up after taking a devastating blow to the jaw. More than anything else, it was his speed that impressed the audience, his ability to dodge the hits as quickly as they came. It was his will to keep fighting, his eagerness to get back up no matter how many times he was beaten down, that terrified me.

The man stopped and examined Avan once more. He was a beast, bulky and muscular, closer to seven feet than to six. His enormous stature made Avan look small.

He smiled. "Avan Gutierrez, young, strong, handsome, resilient. Forty knockouts, ten championships... And one murder."

I felt chilled.

Murder? No! Avan wasn't a killer.

Something rose on Avan's face. Recognition, I thought, but the expression melted into anger so fast that I could've been mistaken. His muscles tensed. His fingers gripped the thick white rope securing him to the beam, his voice nearly a growl.

"You don't know what you're talking about."

"Don't I?" our captor replied, looking at me instead of at Avan. "Maybe I should ask your little girlfriend what she knows."

"He wouldn't do that!" I snapped, struggling against my bonds.

"So. She doesn't know?" he said, not taking his eyes off me. "Boy, you have some explaining to do, aye, Gutierrez? Or maybe I should do the talking for you once I've had my fill of her."

From one heartbeat to the next, Avan's stance changed. I saw his body weight shift, his muscles tense, his grip on the ropes tighten. Using only his arms, he lifted himself and kicked our captor with such force that he fell to the floor, smacking his head against the hardwood floor. He lay, immobile, knocked cold.

Avan twisted and jerked, trying to free himself. I stared down at our captor, not knowing what to think, what to feel.

"This isn't happening," I whispered. "This can't be happening!"

My ears rang, muffling the sounds of Avan's struggles. My entire body went numb.

No one would come looking for us. My parents had practically disowned me, thinking I was demeaning myself by dating an MMA fighter, and hadn't spoken me since I introduced him. Avan's parents were religious fanatics who deemed him 'dammed' for having a relationship outside of marriage. They hadn't contacted him since they'd found out about us. We were on our own now.

"Fuck!" Avan exclaimed, breaking me from my trance.

He was panting now, sweating from the effort. frustration painted across his face. He turned his head and swallowed hard, not looking at me. It took several seconds for him to catch his breath. When he finally did, he sighed and closed his eyes. I'd seen this look before. I saw it after every tap-out. I saw it after every suffocating chokehold. I saw it after every losing match. He was giving up.

What now?

If a mixed martial artist like Avan couldn't break free of his bonds, there was no way in Hell I'd be breaking out of mine.

A low groan made me look down.

"Avan!"

Avan opened his eyes and followed my gaze to our captor, who was slowly coming to. Placing a hand to his head, he rose, unsteady on his feet. Without looking at me or Avan, he stumbled towards the space under the stairs and a mini fridge I hadn't noticed. My heart hammered as I watched him open the door and pull out a needle and vial. Calmly, he stuck the needle into the vial and drew out the clear liquid.

"You made a big mistake, Gutierrez." He snapped his fingers towards the stairs. The door opened and three men came down. One of them carried a black hood. Our captor turned around, smiled and strode towards Avan.

"Hold him still!" he ordered.

The men rushed to Avan, who kicked one to the ground. The other two grabbed hold of him. Avan jerked in their grip.

"Get the fuck off me!"

The third man, the one Avan kicked, got up and joined the others. The more I pulled, the more I fought against the ropes, the tighter the knots became.

"Don't hurt him!" I cried.

Our captor paused. "This won't hurt him," he said, smiling. "It'll just help him relax for a bit while we have our fun."

Avan growled. "You touch her and I'll-"

But he didn't get to finish. With one quick motion, our captor jabbed the needle into Avan's neck and pressed down on the syringe.

Chapter Two

In seconds, I noticed the effect the drug had on Avan. His eyes rolled, his lids growing heavy. His clenched muscles loosened. He shivered under the thick sheen of sweat that gleamed on his dark skin.

"Cut him down."

One of the men pulled a knife from his pocket and cut Avan's wrists free while the other two guided him down. Avan sank to the floor, then rose to his hands and knees, swaying. When he spoke, his words were slurred, breathy, almost inaudible.

"Don't touch her." He sounded drunk out of his mind.

Our captor lifted Avan by the arms and held him there, then turned to me. "Kaine," he said.

I stared at him, confused.

"Call me Kaine," he explained.

Now Avan received my attention. Kaine shoved him to the ground, then laughed when Avan tried to stand and stumbled clumsily to the right. One of the other men caught him before he hit the floor.

"What should we do with 'im?"

Avan's knees gave way, his legs no longer strong enough to support himself. His fingers gripped the long sleeves of the man's sweater. Kaine motioned to the man with the hood. Something in his smile made my stomach drop.

"Let's have some fun."

The hood was pulled over Avan's head as the others turned him around. Although he didn't need them to, Kaine instructed them to hold Avan by each arm. Maybe he was nervous? I couldn't think too long, as Kaine rolled up his sleeves and looked at me, his voice cold.

"This may hurt a little."

I held my breath. Kaine drew back his fist and slammed into Avan's stomach. Avan coughed, his hands closing into fists for a fraction of a second as he fought for air.

"No, please!" I begged. "Stop!"

Kaine didn't hesitate, becoming more violent as the beating continued. Avan was shoved to the floor. They took turns, all four of them, alternating between punching and kicking, giving Avan no time to recover. Tears pricked at the corners of my eyes as Avan fought to speak, to move, to do anything. He wouldn't be able to fight against the drugs for too much longer.

This is it. This is how Avan is going to die.

AVAN LOWERED HIMSELF slowly into the tub of warm water.

"Did you really have to add the bubbles?" he asked with a light laugh.

I sat on the stool nearest to him and smiled.

"It's lavender, jerk!" I said, giving his shoulder a playful shove. "It's supposed to be relaxing."

He smiled warmly at me, laid his head back against the towel behind him and closed his eyes. "Thank you."

I didn't respond. Really, the suds that covered his battered body were there for me. I wasn't with him when he got undressed and I wouldn't be with him when he got out. It was the sight of the bruises, the marks which brought me back to the grueling hours of training, to the brutality of the fights. The marks I couldn't bear to look at.

"Hey."

I felt a wet hand on mine and lifted my gaze to meet his.

"You okay?"

I forced a smile, something I was doing more and more often. I took his fingers gently in my own and kissed his bruised knuckles. He made a face. I could see that somehow, he knew. He'd known what was wrong all along.

"What can I do to make it better?" he asked.

His green eyes were full of the concern I loved so much. I took a deep breath and sat on the edge of the tub.

"Take out the trash, do the dishes, maybe vacuum the carpets every once in a while."

He chuckled at my sarcasm. I raised my eyebrows, trying to keep a straight face.

"I'm serious, Avan."

He laughed again, and wrapped an arm around my waist. His wet thumb brushed my hip, making me shiver.

"Oh, you're serious, huh?"

I closed my eyes and looked away, hiding my growing smile. "Yes, I a-"

I was cut short when I felt myself being pulled into the tub. My hands slipped as I grabbed for the side for support, but to no avail. I splashed into the silky water with a gasp. Avan wrapped his arms around me, holding me to him as I wiggled and squirmed and laughed so hard it hurt.

"Where you goin', huh? " he said, giggling. "Why you trying to get away from me?"

He tickled my sides and I surrendered.

"Okay, okay!" I said, catching my breath.

His arms around me loosened and I looked over the edge of the bathtub. Soapy water was everywhere.

"You're cleaning this up." I whispered, leaning back against him.

He kissed my ear. "You're a terrible liar."

I gave a little giggle and sank deeper into the water, sighing when I felt Avan pull me tighter to his chest. I leaned against his shoulder and breathed him in, sighing once more. Being in his arms was like being wrapped in a blanket that had just been taken out of the dryer. He was so warm. These were the moments which made it all worthwhile, these times of peace and distraction, away from the cage, away from the blood, away from the violence. These were the moments that held me together when I felt certain I would break apart.

Avan took a deep breath and I sighed in frustration, knowing he would break the silence, that this moment wouldn't last forever.

"You know, you don't need to worry about me. I'm-"

"Yes, I know that you're fine. I know that!" I snapped at him. God, why? Why did he have to ruin it like that? "I'm sorry," I said, rubbing my face with wet hands. "It's just hard."

He leaned his cheek onto my hair. "What is?"

I sniffed and wiped at my tears. There was a still-healing wound on his forearm, one I hadn't noticed until now. It was swollen and red and painful. My voice was suddenly small.

"Seeing you like this. Seeing you so sore you can't even tie your own shoes. All of those bruises and the swelling, and the blo-" I shivered in the warm water. "I should be used to it by now, but I'm not. Maybe I never will be."

Avan's chest shuddered. "What can I do?" he whispered, pressing his lips to my hair. "How can I help?"

I didn't dare speak the words resting on my lips. Telling him to stop fighting was like telling an artist to stop painting or a writer to stop writing or a human to stop breathing. Mixed Martial Arts was his passion. I saw it in the thrill of a victory and the devastation of a loss. Fighting was as much a part of him as every beat of his heart, and I had no right to take it away. I swallowed my disappointment, a sour mouthful, and closed my eyes.

"Sing to me."

He kissed my hair, paused for a moment, and then kissed my cheek, lightly. My beautiful distraction. His voice was a quiet whisper near my ear.

"Don't worry / About a thing / Cuz, every little thing / Is gonna be alright...."

AVAN WASN'T MOVING. He lay on his side, moaning softly and trying to speak. Kaine panted, sweating as though the beating had taken everything out of him.

"He'll be hurting for a couple of weeks," he sneered. He crouched beside Avan's hooded face. "If you try anything else, she'll be next."

Avan's fingers flexed. His breathing became short and shallow. My chest ached at the sight of him. So vulnerable. So defeated.

"And you," our captor said, standing and walking towards me. He pulled out a pocket knife and began cutting my binds. "You'll behave, won't you? You don't want anything else happening to him, do you?"

"I'll behave," I said, in a voice I fought to keep steady. "I promise."

He smiled at me. "Good girl."

I sat up and rubbed my sore wrists as the three stooges unplugged the little fridge and carried it up the stairs. When I was certain they were gone, hearing the door lock, I rushed to Avan. I knelt beside him, hesitating to remove the sack from his head.

"Don't break down," I mouthed to myself. "Avan needs you."

Slowly, carefully, I pulled the sack from his head. A few strands of dark curls fell over his cheek and eyes. I brushed them back behind his ear and winced at the blood, because of the swelling that stood out on his cheekbone. He looked at me without moving his head. His eye had already started to blacken, blood dripping from the corner where the skin had broken. His bottom lip was split open. I couldn't bear to think about the wounds that lay hidden under his clothes. He smiled weakly at me, trying to sound strong. His voice was slurred, weak, broken.

"I'm ok-ay..." He trailed off, his eyes rolling. They closed, and he went completely limp.

"No, no, no, no!" I frantically tapped my hands against his cheeks. "Avan, wake up. Come on. Please!"

I hit him harder, smacking him on the cheek. His eyes sprang open and he winced, inhaling sharply. My fingers covered my mouth briefly before they were back on Avan's face.

"God, I'm sorry! I'm sorry, Avan. Just stay awake, baby. You have to stay awake." I stroked my fingers through his hair, and wiped away the blood I could from his face with the sleeves of my shirt.

He blinked, trying to speak again, but I shushed him. He groaned helplessly as his eyes rolled again. My blood ran cold before I remembered the drugs in his veins. They must've been taking their full effect, leaving Avan slipping in and out of consciousness.

"It'll wear off," I assured him, or maybe it was me needing the reassurance. "But until it does, I'm here for you, okay?"

I repositioned myself on the floor, cradling his head in my lap, my fingers tracing the faint outline of stubble along his jaw. There was blood in his goatee. When he spoke again, his words came in a tired, breathy whisper, his eyes opening.

"Sing to me."

My eyes filled with tears. I swallowed and sang the song that we loved so much, the melody barely above a whisper.

"Don't worry / About a thing / Cuz, every little thing / Is gonna be alright...."

Chapter Three

I stayed with him, keeping him awake and with me in the moment, as both of us waited for the drugs to wear off.

It's funny what the mind will do under stress to distract itself. My eyes crawled over the room, taking in the warm colors I hadn't noticed before. The floor, like the walls, was made of a cherry-red wood. The carpet beneath the bed was orange and the bedclothes rose red. There was a bathroom, too, which seemed to be a cozy little space. Even the bed was comfortable, the blanket silky and soft, shining in the dim light of the bedside lamps. The light reflected off the walls too, and the floors, making everything look clean. Every inch of this basement was a warm color. And I loved it despite the predicament we were in.

I want a basement like this one day, I thought.

I really did. This cozy feeling was appealing to me. The warmth of the colors and dimness of the lamps reminded me of fall. It brought me back to lazy winter days spent with my brother, playing video games, drinking hot cocoa and watching scary movies as the snow fell in a thick blanket outside.

Days I missed.

Slowly, Avan's leg drew closer to his body.

"Avan, thank God." My heart pounded with anxiety and relief. His eyes focused on me. He whispered my name questioningly.

"I'm here, baby." I soothed. "You're okay." I wasn't at all sure if that last part was true. "Are you in pain?"

He didn't answer but rose groggily, a hand placed to his head. His face changed, as if realizing where we were and what had happened. He clutched my shoulders suddenly, almost angrily. I flinched, startled by the fierceness in his eyes.

"Did they hurt you?"

It took me a moment to process exactly what he meant. Yes, they had hurt me. They had hurt me by hurting him, but that wasn't what Avan was asking. He was asking if they'd *touched* me. If they'd violated me. If they took advantage of me while he was down.

I shook my head, wondering why. The men hadn't touched me. Why? Avan was completely vulnerable. He couldn't have stopped them even if he wanted to. The men had to have known that. Yet they didn't touch me. Why?

Avan started searching for a way out.

I didn't think there was a way out. The basement was windowless. The door was padlocked; I'd heard the distinctive clack and clank when they'd left us here. Still, there was no point in explaining to Avan. His determination, his will, was like a runaway train, impossible to stop. He'd argue against the falling of night, and he'd search for an escape. Unlike me, his optimism would insist there was a way out.

I got up and silently retreated to the bed. I sat cross-legged, absentmindedly pulling threads from the knees of my jeans, and watched Avan scour the basement restlessly. He looked for windows. He rummaged through the drawers in the bathroom and nightstands, coming up empty. He paced, linking his hands behind his head. He ignored my presence completely.

Only when he started yelling, rushing up the stairs and kicking the door with his bare foot, that I jumped from the bed and attempted to calm him. I ventured up the stairs and put my hands on him. His normally soft, gentle voice was vicious and hateful.

"Come on, motherfuckers!"

What the Hell was he doing? Wasn't he afraid of being drugged and beaten again? Or beaten even worse? No, of course he wasn't. But I was.

"Avan, stop!"

He didn't listen. He continued kicking, yelling, slamming his shoulder into the door. This wasn't him, this desperate creature.

"Avan, calm down!" I grabbed his arm, but he tore away from me. He paced the room again, linking his fingers through his hair, breathing so hard I was sure he was growling.

"There's no way out, Avan." I walked slowly down the stairs. It was a harsh truth, but it was still the truth.

Avan didn't want to accept it, but I saw it spread across his face. Finally, he made a terrible noise, a sound of defeat, before sliding his back down one of the walls and sitting on the floor, his head low. I settled beside him, sinking back on my heels. After a long moment, he wrapped an arm around me, pulling me closer. His free hand lifted to his mouth, stayed there for a short while, then slowly slid down his chin.

I knew this gesture; it was a sign of stress. Without saying anything, I took his fingers in my own, brought them to my lips and held them there, wondering what he was thinking. My eyes lingered on his bloody shirt, following the red trail to his neck and mouth. Blood was smeared on his cheeks where I'd tried to wipe it away. Pink abrasions covered his hands and arms. Rough scabs covered several small cuts to his face. One wound stood out amongst the rest: the bloody cut to the corner of his eye.

"That looks bad."

He raised his fingers to his eye, feeling at the clot of dried blood, and my eyes found the split in his bottom lip again. I stood and held my hand out to him. He took it and rose, following me, docile, all fight vanished like a puddle in the sun.

"Shirt off." I said when we got into the bathroom.

Avan sat on the edge of the tub, his fingers gripping the sides. "You're awfully bossy, ya know?" he teased, smiling.

I smiled back at him, grateful for his teasing. I didn't bother looking for disinfectant. I just dampened a washcloth I'd found on the counter and sat on the closed toilet lid.

"Shirt off." I said again, tugging it over his stomach. Though I didn't need to, I helped him ease it off, then glanced away without turning my head. His chest and stomach were covered with dark patches, painful bruises tinted with deep purples and reds.

"Don't freak out," he said, soothingly.

I swallowed. My eyes flitted to his. "Do they hurt as bad as they look?"

Avan shrugged, unfazed. "Nah, it's not bad. I've been through worse." He forced a smile, causing the clot on his lip to tear and bleed. I dabbed at the blood.

I knew he was right. He put his body on the line every time he stepped foot into the cage or into the gym for a sparring session. He was used to it, conditioned for the beating he chose to endure. Kaine's attack, as vicious as it was, was nothing compared to what Avan trained for. Even when he came out of a fight uninjured, the weeks of vigorous training left him so sore and exhausted that giving him a hug required caution and restraint.

But he was wrong, too. I could sense the tension in his body, hear the tightness in his voice. The beating had affected him far more than he led on, but Avan, being the fighter that he was, tried to hide it.

"What does he want with us?"

Avan lowered his eyes. He shrugged his shoulders. He looked like a little kid being forced to confess to a naughty deed he'd done. I frowned and wiped at the deep cut in the corner of his eye with a feather-light touch.

"Why you?"

Avan looked at me. Why was he looking at me? I hadn't said it out loud. Or had I?

My cheeks felt hot. Avan's eyes seemed to melt before me. They gleamed and appeared softer and greener than ever.

"I'm glad it was me."

He didn't explain, but I knew. He meant the rebellion, the beating, the example. I thought about what would've happened if I'd been the one who'd stood up to the men. I thought about how easily they could've drugged and beaten me instead. And how much further they could have gone. The very thought of it, the vision of it in my head, made my skin crawl. I was suddenly thankful that it had been Avan who took the beating.

And I was ashamed.

I made a motion for Avan to give me his arm and he did. Neither of us said anything more as I tended to the abrasions and the rest of his wounds. Maybe there wasn't anything left to say.

Chapter Four

For four days, we were left in the basement. For four days, Avan searched for a way out as his body healed. For four days, we were left without food. We got our water from the tap.

Avan sat with his back against the bed. I sat with him, straining my ears to hear the muffled conversations upstairs.

Finally, Avan looked at me, eyes glistening, face etched with sadness. "I need to tell you something."

He sounded guilty, as he almost always did, but what was there to feel guilty about? In the two years I'd known him, he'd been nothing but kind to me and those around him. He never snapped at me when he was having a rough day, nor had he treated me with anything less than respect and unconditional love. What could he possibly feel guilty about?

I sat quietly, waiting for him to say more, but the door to the basement unlocked. I heard the padlock rattle, then clank against the hasp before being pulled away. At the sound of heavy boots coming down the stairs, Avan clutched me tighter, as if our captors would try to snatch me and run.

Kaine carried a small stool. He placed it in front of us. "I'll make you a deal, Gutierrez," he said, sitting down. "And I suggest you agree. It's the least you could do."

Avan's grip around me loosened and his face softened. His green eyes, glistening with tears, slid to Kaine's face, then away again.

"What's the deal?"

Kaine smiled and Avan blinked his tears away before they had the chance to fall. I had a sickening feeling that there was an unspoken secret between them, something I knew nothing about. Not the supposed murder. I knew that was a lie. It had to be.

Kaine spoke slowly, as if wanting to be sure we understood. "I want $50,000."

A look of surprise crossed Avan's face.

"You're a gifted man, Gutierrez, so here's the deal. You help me raise the money and I'll grant you two your freedom. Does that seem fair?"

From the tone of his voice, I knew he wasn't talking about a lemonade stand. God, what was he going to make us do? Sell our bodies? Become drug dealers? Something worse? What could possibly be worse?

"If you don't comply," Kaine continued, taking his knife from his pocket. "I guess I'll be forced to have my way with her. Maybe leave her body on the side of the road when I'm done."

Avan's arms suddenly tightened around me, squeezing me so hard that it almost hurt.

"Leave her out of this," he spat. "I'll do whatever you want. Just leave her alone!"

I wanted to say something, anything that would keep Avan from agreeing to something dangerous, but I didn't. I wasn't brave enough to speak up. I sat in Avan's arms and kept my mouth shut, feeling sorry for myself because I was a coward.

A row of yellow teeth flashed in Kaine's grin. He took Avan's shirt and threw it aside. He snapped his fingers and the three other men came down the stairs with hoods, zip-ties and a pair of shorts. This wasn't good. Kaine took the shorts and handed them to Avan.

"Put these on."

Avan didn't protest. He stood up, undid his ties and dropped his pants. I felt a rush of fear pass through me in a wave of pins and needles. They were basketball shorts, the baggy comfortable sort you slip on before going to play a game with friends. But something told me that our captors weren't looking for a friendly game of hoops. Something told me it would be worse.

And it was.

Bound at knife point and blinded with hoods, Avan and I were taken upstairs and forced out of the house. I shivered in the freezing air and knew Avan was shivering too. In fact, he had it worse. I had my clothes and shoes. I thought of Avan's bare feet and chest in this frigid weather. It was almost impossible to resist the urge to stop walking and wrap my arms around him. I couldn't comfort him even if I wanted to.

I spooked at the sudden rumble of a truck engine. A faintly familiar scent flooded into my nostrils, sweet and sharp. It was the smell of pine trees, lots of them. We had to be near a forest. Images of Avan and I being beaten, tortured, thrown into the woods, and left for dead flashed through my mind. I couldn't do this. I wouldn't do this.

My legs gave way. My feet skidded in the snow as I tried to keep myself from being taken any further. For a moment, for a split second, I didn't think about what might happen to Avan. I thought of only my own will to escape, to survive, to live.

It was futile. As soon as the men realized I wasn't moving any further, I was hit in the face and lifted off the ground.

Dazed, and sitting in the truck, I felt a warm trickle of blood sliding down my cheek. How stupid I'd been to think I could run through the woods bound and blindfolded. How stupid I'd been to think I could just run off, and...

And leave Avan behind to face the wrath alone.

My head whirled. I moaned and put my head down on my knees, overcome with hatred for myself.

I shuddered when the door beside me opened, letting in a blast of icy wind. Avan was shoved into me with such force that I was pushed to the other side of the truck. Then the door slammed shut and it was Avan and I, sitting in silence.

Chapter Five

I ce crunched beneath the tires as the truck came to a stop.

No, no, no, no!

I wanted to break free of my zip-ties, take Avan's hand, tell him how much he meant to me, apologize for not being braver. I couldn't; I wasn't strong enough. Instead, I shuffled across the seats until I felt his shoulder pressed against mine. I buried my face against him. He pressed his mouth hard against my head. We sat there, one soul in two bodies, waiting for the end.

The door beside us opened and Avan was dragged out before I could say goodbye. Then it was my turn. I kicked and thrashed with everything I had, my muscles burning with the effort. All around me, voices were raised in malice, anger, and frustration. A pair of arms grabbed me from behind, holding me firmly in place. My hood was removed. Hot breath blew over my ear.

"Don't make this difficult," a male voice growled.

He pointed to where Avan stood, restrained by Kaine. His back arched in a painful position, and I could see the deadly gleam of the blade of a knife held to the smooth skin of his throat. The message was clear. I accepted my defeat and moved as I was directed.

It took me a while to realize we weren't in the woods, or even a remote area. We were in a parking lot with two or three cars, not counting the truck. Where there were cars, there were people. Tears welled up in my eyes. We weren't going to die.

Not yet.

We were led to a warehouse, old and ramshackle, like it hadn't been used in years. A few feet away from the door, Kaine cut Avan's bonds and he stumbled forward, back curled, arms spread as if to keep himself from falling. The knife was tossed to my guard and my bonds were cut too. I rushed away before they could stop me, crashing into Avan. I felt his hands in my hair as he pressed me closer. I could feel the heat of his body fitting perfectly with my own, even through my clothes. I soaked in his warmth.

He pushed away from me, stared at my face for a moment, then wiped the blood from my cheek with his hand. I'd been so focused on my emotions throughout the ride, I hadn't noticed the throbbing pain on the right side of my face. I felt it now as I lifted a hand to my cheek and winced. Avan's eyebrows drew closer together. I saw a blazing fire destroying the lush forests in his eyes. Anticipating his next move, I grabbed his arm.

"Avan, don't!"

He didn't listen. He tore his arm from mine, turned, and rushed at Kaine. The other two men barely corralled him, grasping his arms as he barreled past. They held him back as he struggled and grunted, teeth bared like a snarling wolf. Steam clouded around his mouth as soon as it hit the air.

"If you ever touch her again-"

"Easy, Gutierrez!" one of the men interrupted. "We're the ones with the knife."

Kaine laughed and shook his head. Avan's face didn't change. The crease in his brow worsened. I couldn't let his temper, his protectiveness, get him hurt again. My voice was low but unyielding.

"Avan, please."

Slowly, Avan's body relaxed. His breathing steadied, his snarl wiped away. Kaine laughed again and herded us towards the giant metal doors, keeping the knife close. The doors were opened and my breath caught. I saw the cage before I saw anything else. It was massive, nearly taking up the entire bottom of the two-story building.

Of all the scenarios that tumbled around in my head as we approached the warehouse, this wasn't one of them.

Chapter Six

“Take off your shirt.”

Avan stood in the doorway of our bedroom, his shirt darkened by sweat, his long curly hair tied back in a messy bun. He'd been out for most of the morning, jogging, while I cleaned the house and prepared a late brunch for us.

“Oohh, kinky,” he breathed, rushing out of his sleeves.

I stood on my toes and kissed his chapped lips, taking the shirt as I did. He leaned in and kissed me back, his teeth grazing my lower lip. I shivered and pushed him gently away.

“Slow your roll there,” I whispered, smiling at his hungry eyes. “I'm just doing laundry.”

He laughed, small and silent, and stepped out of the way. He was still shirtless when I returned from the laundry room, empty basket in hand. Glancing at his figure, I paused by our bed when I saw a large patch of color on his back. I squinted harder into the bathroom where he washed his face at the sink. A tattoo I'd never seen before rested on his shoulder blade, an outline of irritated skin surrounding it, indicating that it was new, or newish. Avan's eyes found my reflection in the mirror. He frowned.

“Do you hate it?” he asked me, almost guiltily.

It took me a long while to answer. I wasn't against tattoos. On the contrary, I had a few of them myself: a semi colon for my brother on the inside of my wrist, his jersey number beneath it, the date of his birth behind my right ear, the date of his death *behind the other, his full name across my lower back. It was that —normally— Avan didn't specifically show me his new tats, like a child showing his mother the straight A's on his report card. He'd wait until I saw it, or casually point it out, because it wasn't a big deal. But he hadn't shown me this one or even mentioned that he got it.*

I abandoned the laundry basket, strode behind him, and wrapped my arms around his flat stomach. Taking in the musky scent that wafted off him, I pressed my lips to his back.

"I love it."

Avan turned around to face me.

"Really?"

I smiled, leaning into him. I wasn't the type of girl to get angry at her boyfriend for getting body art without my permission. I'd done it often enough without my mother's permission, so who was I to judge Avan?

"Yes, really."

His hands slid to my waist, his thumbs hooking into the loops of my shorts.

I sighed, fighting the longing, the wanting that plagued me. It took everything to not give in to our desires. I rested my chin on his shoulder and studied the new tattoo reflected in the mirror. It was breathtaking. Its beautiful, intricate lines formed the delicate body of a monarch butterfly, the colors vibrant and bright against the olive tones of Avan's skin.

"Why a butterfly?" I asked, raising an eyebrow.

He unhooked his thumbs from my shorts. His fingers traced desire on the bare skin of my thighs. My skin tightened into goosebumps.

"Why not?"

I shrugged, my chin still on his shoulder.

"I just figured a guy like you would get something a little more, oh, I don't know. Manly? Like a skull or a hatchet or something."

Avan suddenly pulled back. He tried to sound offended, but I knew him well enough to detect the playfulness in his voice.

"So, I'm not manly enough for you, huh?" His arms wrapped tightly around me. He grunted as if it took all his strength to lift me off my feet and out of the bathroom.

"Avan, come on, put me down!" I laughed.

He lowered me to the bed, his hands pinning my arms onto the blankets. My heart raced as he straddled me, trapping me beneath him.

"Is this manly enough for you?" he asked, voice taunting and low.

I giggled as I admitted I couldn't think of a better word. He flashed a crooked smile, leaned in, and gave me the lightest of kisses.

"Butterflies symbolize rebirth, a second chance to —to do things right."

I frowned at him and spoke my next words slowly. "What have you done wrong?"

His body stiffened, his flirtatious mood shattered. He swallowed, his face turning slightly away from mine. He released my arms, placing his hands beside them instead, looking more hurt than guilty now. Staring off at nothing, his mind was in a world I wasn't allowed to be in. The pain in his face, the way his lip quivered, his green eyes shining with tears - it killed me. For the first time, it hit me. Seeing him in emotional pain was far worse than knowing he was in physical pain.

I regretted asking the question. Whatever he'd done in the past, if he said it was bad? It was bad. But that was the key word: past. Even if he'd done something horrible, he wasn't that person anymore. He was always so gentle with me, almost as careful as I was when tending his injuries after a fight.

His kindness extended beyond our home. He demonstrated selflessness toward his opponents after every winning fight: extending a hand to help them to their feet after a submission, crouching to ensure they regained consciousness after a knockout, lifting their legs as they lay unmoving on the canvas. As naive as it might have been, I didn't need to wonder what he'd done. I didn't care.

"You don't need to talk about anything you don't want to," I said, touching his chin. "Not with me."

He looked at me, eyes teary, relief written all over his face. "Do you know how much I love you?"

"Why don't you show me?" I whispered back.

He Inhaled heavily, took my face in his hands, and pulled me into the most passionate kiss we'd ever shared. My whole being felt drawn to his mouth. His tongue, his touch, teasing and tempting me, reminded me of our past, promising, no, demanding more. I gasped, my stomach contracting with excitement. My hands ran from his chest and downward, tracing every muscle my fingers could find, loving the way his body trembled and tightened, knowing I was helping him forget whatever was hurting him. We sat, our bodies controlled by invisible strings, our breaths synced, our minds focused only on what the other needed.

His soft hands slid inside my shirt, his long fingers mapping a course along the curves of my breasts, my belly, my hips, everywhere I loved being touched. Before I knew it, my shirt was *off, my bra unhooked. We fell back onto the bed in a tangle of arms and bare skin, kicking off our shorts, getting closer and closer, seeking almost to be drawn into each other. He kissed me up and down, lips searing my toes, my knees, my thighs. One hand spread my legs as his mouth crawled up my body, his skin brushing against mine. My fingers dug into his shoulders, wanting him closer but he resisted, his fighter's body denying my desire.*

"Avan," I half-whispered, half-moaned, and he silenced me with another of his kisses, melting into me. I didn't know how long he lingered, how long he toyed with me. It could have been minutes, it could have been days. It felt like an eternity and I never wanted it to end. Finally, finally, he centered himself over me, gazing into my eyes. "I love you," he said, as he lowered himself onto me, my skin screaming for his touch.

I moaned softly, my toes curling as a wave of warmth and pressure washed through me. All at once I felt everything, every nerve afire, as he slowly, oh my god so slowly, slid into me, then rested there. He smiled down, a sweet smile, and I smiled back.

"Like this?" he asked, and moved ever so slightly.

"Avan," is all I could manage.

"Yes or no," he insisted, stilling again.

"Yes," I hissed. "Now."

His smile turned into a grin as he started to move, my body tingling with every slow thrust of his hips. He caressed me in ways that filled me with a sense of absolute safety, absolute security, and I surrendered myself to him, to the moment. Every sensation left me acutely aware of everything he did, of the way his hands cradled my face when he kissed me, the way he looked at me with deep tenderness, the way he touched me as if my body was made of glass.

I knew, in that moment, that he would never let anyone hurt me. I was his world and he was mine. I moaned louder, running my fingers through his hair, giving fully to him at last.

AVAN WAS PUSHED INTO the octagon, the cage door locked behind him. Kaine forced me into the crowd that had gathered in the minutes after we arrived. Men were setting up kegs of beer in a corner. Teenagers were fist-bumping before taking bets on which fighter would come out on top. Others engaged in shadowboxing.

Nothing was said about the scabs and bruises on Avan's face and body. The men and boys looked at him with respect. Wounds were something to be admired here, a sign that one had put up a good fight, an assumption that Avan had held his own.

Avan's opponent, a muscular man who looked more like he lifted weights rather than ran, stood at the other side of the cage. He was a bear to Avan's panther, blocky where Avan was lithe, and cocky, gesturing wildly to himself to get the crowd's attention. He pointed at Avan, taunting him, poking fun at his longer hair and leaner frame.

This beast didn't stand a chance.

From Avan, I'd learned that large muscles were unimportant in MMA and seen evidence of that in his workouts. He was always running, jumping, sparring, focusing on his agility and stamina rather than how much he could bench press. Physical strength in the cage wasn't as crucial as the ability to move swiftly and stay off one's back. Still, anything could happen in the cage. One bad kick could change everything. Although I knew Avan had the upper hand in this fight, my skin still pricked with anxiety.

"There are no rules here," Kaine whispered, ratcheting up my anxiety. I swallowed. My skin crawled as Kaine held me firmly by the shoulders. With one quick motion of the hand, the fight began.

Chapter Seven

A jab to the nose was all it took for the blood to flow.

It was Avan who threw the punch. I saw it happen through gaps between my fingers.

I watched.

I didn't watch.

My fingers stayed clasped over my eyes, hiding all but Avan's head and upper body. I kept my eyes on him, not on the crowd that pounded him with profanity, not on his opponent. He was suffering under the weight of his muscles as Avan dodged his strikes, his lean figure moving gracefully out of the way. He moved as quickly as the punches were thrown, his feet carrying him effortlessly across the canvas. The bigger man looked weary as blood gushed from his nose, and he had a right to be. Avan's strikes were fierce, but his kicks were even fiercer.

For an instant, nothing happened. I watched Avan's eyes dart back and forth, thinking and visualizing his next move. Then he leaped upward, his body twisting to the right as his left leg straightened. His shin caught the shoulder of his opponent, sending the man falling onto the canvas.

I winced, remembering the time I'd cracked my shin on the leg of a table while rushing for the phone. The pain was immediate, a sharp searing heat that forced me to the floor. Tears filled my eyes and I couldn't stop the small cry that fell from my lips.

The pain that Avan was feeling had to have been worse, bone on bone. Yet when he landed expertly back on his feet, Avan shook it off, bouncing lightly on the balls of his feet until the pain subsided, until his opponent rose unsteadily and charged. He locked his arms around Avan's waist and slammed him back against the cage.

I winced again, wanting to look away, but unable to. Avan's arms were up, his elbows down, shielding his nose and eyes from the blows that rained down on him.

"Break 'im!" one of the spectators yelled from behind me. "He's hurt! Go for the ribs!"

Somehow the beast heard over the din, delivering his strikes to Avan's abused rib cage and body. Relentlessly, that's where they stayed. A bitter lump of anguish rose in my throat as I watched Avan struggle to stay upright, his teeth and muscles clenched.

"Come on, Avan," I mouthed, wringing my hands. "Get out of there."

Avan's body curled helplessly forward, whether from instinct or the beating, I didn't know. His knees buckled. My eyes followed him to the ground. Sitting against the cage, he curled into a ball and received a torrent of punches, most of them to his head. I whimpered softly, a cry rising in my throat. A chuckle came from behind me and my cheeks burned hot.

How was this funny? What sort of monster would laugh at someone who was completely defenseless being beaten?

Of course I knew who it was. It was Kaine. I couldn't see him, but I knew he'd laughed. I wasn't the type of person who got joy out of hurting people, but I wanted nothing more than to turn and claw his eyes out at that moment.

I pushed down my rage and focused on Avan. During my brief lapse of attention, Avan had recovered and somehow managed to pin his opponent to the canvas. Now he had a hold of his opponent's arm, his legs extended across the man's broad chest to gain leverage, turning his hip on the elbow, forcing the joint outside its normal range of motion. The man's face reddened, his expression pained as Avan twisted his hip further. Within a few seconds, the man tapped out.

Avan rose to his feet and extended his hand to his opponent, who lay stunned, disappointed, defeated, his nose still bleeding. He slapped Avan's hand away, stood up, and walked to the other side of the wide cage, holding his nose. Avan didn't celebrate. He didn't raise his arms or smile at the crowd or run around the inside of the octagon. Instead, he sighed and linked his hands behind his head, turning away and pulling at his hair.

Sweat glistened on his back and shoulders in a way I very strangely loved to watch. I could just barely make out the pink outline of the cage on his back. His shoulders rose and fell with each heaving breath, the butterfly tattoo rising with them. For a full minute, that's all he did, walked aimlessly around the center of the cage while his opponent received treatment for his broken nose.

These weren't doctors, the men treating him. I knew because I remembered the first time I'd seen Avan break his nose during a fight. Four men surrounded him and worked with a sense of quickness and urgency, snapping it back into place. They then tilted his head back and dabbed away the blood with a warm wet cloth.

The two men tending to Avan's opponent were utterly clueless. When the next round started, it was evident they hadn't attempted to put the crooked mess of cartilage back to its original position, though they'd managed to stop the bleeding.

No one came to tend to Avan. Though this was something I half expected given the heartlessness of our captor, inside I seethed with rage. When the first punch was thrown, this time by Avan's opponent, I let the anger show. I opened my mouth, my words spilling out before I could clamp a hand over my lips.

"Take 'im down, Babe!"

Had I really said that? Had Avan even heard me? Why was I suddenly itching to see his opponent hurt?

This wasn't me. I knew with all my heart it wasn't, but there was no taking the words back now. Avan *had* heard me because he'd turned his head for a second and flashed his quick, crooked smile in my direction. I turned my eyes away, my hand over my mouth, feeling heartless and cruel. Watching Avan sustain brutal injuries during a fight was unbearable, so why did I want to see the same thing happen to his opponent? *Why?*

A loud thud tore me from my thoughts.

Shifting my attention back to the cage, I saw Avan getting up, red dripping from his mouth. He wiped his lips with his hand, smearing blood across his face. I shuddered, my stomach twisting and churning.

Avan didn't falter. He jumped again, spinning midair and catching his opponent's cheek with the heel of his foot, following it with a strike that sent the man staggering back and left Avan shaking off the pain in his hand.

I realized with a jolt that they didn't have handwraps, and they needed them! Without them, a fighter could easily break a finger or even a hand, tear a tendon, even cause permanent damage. This was why they were so crucial in MMA, why Avan needed to wear them even in training.

Avan shrugged his shoulders, as if pushing past the damage, and went for another kick, dropping his opponent to his knees, his face shocked. A Liver Kick was what they called it. I knew from watching Avan that no fighter, no matter how fast, strong, or experienced, could withstand this devastating blow.

The beast's legs buckled beneath him. He collapsed, folding into himself for several seconds. The kick had left him completely incapacitated.

Kaine had underestimated Avan. Avan may have been thin, lanky, and not nearly as muscular as the man who knelt before him, but he wasn't stupid. As much as his smaller size and lightning speed helped him in the cage, it was his quick thinking that made him deadly. His ability to assess and act on a situation in a single breath gave him the advantage in these rounds.

Avan set upon his opponent, wrapping his arms around the man's torso. They struggled on the ground, Avan fighting to get a good grip on him and his opponent scrambling to get away. They slipped in the spots of blood they dripped. The stuff was everywhere now, dark and thick against the off-white of the canvas. I clasped my hands.

"Come on, Avan," I whispered, closing my eyes. "Take him down!"

When I opened my eyes, Avan was lying behind the man, one arm wrapped around his throat, the other arm pushing on the back of his head in a chokehold, and both legs around his waist. As I watched, I read Avan's lips.

"Tap out, man! Tap out!"

If it weren't for the screaming crowd, I'd probably have heard him. But the crowd was screaming, screaming so loud that my ears rang. I should've been glad, because they were screaming for Avan. As quickly as they'd cheered the beast, now we were all anxious to see him win. Though there was one more round he'd have to endure, we became hysterical when his opponent tapped his fingers on the canvas.

Avan rolled onto his back and covered his face with his hands. Panting, the beast stood and walked to his corner, rubbing his throat, his neck red, his body stiff.

But Avan didn't move. He stayed where he was, breathing just as heavily, his hands still hiding his face. I would've given anything to know what he was thinking, what he was feeling. Finally, he rose, wiping the remaining blood from his mouth and chin.

I had to convince myself that the blood was from his mouth that had stopped bleeding, and not from his hand, which was smeared with it. Avan walked in tight circles with his hands behind his head. Again, rage filled me, but the final round began before I could put it into words or action.

The beast was exhausted, sweating, out of breath. He wouldn't last much longer.

I knew this.

Avan knew this. He kept his distance, making the beast come to him to throw a punch or a kick. The beast tired quickly. He slipped in the blood that covered the floor of the cage, stumbling and falling. Avan seized his chance, climbing on top of the beast and placing him in a knee bar. It was enough to make him tap and submit.

The beast was down. Avan had won!

For the second time, Avan extended a hand and for the second time, the beast refused it. Avan walked off, to the door of the cage. I broke out of Kaine's grip and pushed through the crowd to get to the stairs.

When the cage was unlocked and Avan stepped out, I didn't scan his body for wounds. I didn't even try to restrain myself. I threw my arms around him and wept tears of relief into his shoulder. He pulled me closer, his hand cradling the back of my head. For a long time, I could hear nothing but his ragged breathing and my heartbeat.

Despite the cocoon we tried to create, I knew Kaine stood behind us. I thought I could feel Avan staring at him, green eyes angry, expression menacing as his arms wrapped me in a protective grip.

Chapter Eight

The basement was colder than when we left. As soon as we were freed, our hoods taken off and the zip-ties cut, I guided a freezing Avan to the bed. I sat him down and wrapped the blanket and sheets around his shoulders. He shivered uncontrollably as I crouched in front of him, taking his hands and gathering them to my chest. His teeth chattered, his face downcast as if not wanting me to notice. Sweat was frozen to his hair. His fingers and toes were as frigid as the rest of him.

I drew our knotted fingers to my mouth and breathed on them, rubbing his palms and fingers to get them warm. His knuckles were bloodied and bruised. Dried blood crusted his gathering goatee, its metallic scent still on his breath. But it was the sight of his ribs, dark purple and ugly, which hurt worst.

"My poor baby," I whispered.

He looked at me, finally warm enough to stop shivering, but he didn't pull his hands away. Instead, he leaned forward, closed his eyes, and rested his forehead against mine. I felt his brow crease as he sighed. The scent of blood was stronger now.

Say something. Please, Avan. I thought these words but didn't speak, unwilling to break the silence first. He hadn't said one word to me since we'd been forced into the truck. Before this moment, I took his voice for granted. Now, I craved it, and his prolonged silence scared me.

He pulled back, his eyes steady on me, and I sat beside him on the bed, crossing my legs. His hands pulled from mine and touched my cheek, his fingers still ice cold. When I flinched, he stood up, taking my hand and letting the blanket fall back onto the bed.

"Let's get you cleaned up," he said, very quietly.

Me? Why was he worried about me? It didn't seem possible. He was the one who was forced into the cage, the one who'd endured three rounds of constant, painful exertion, the one who'd slipped on his blood in the octagon. Yet here he was, sitting me on the edge of the tub.

Looking in the mirror, I was shocked to find my face looking as battered as Avan's. The entire right side, where Kaine's fist struck me, was red and puffy to the point where my eye had blackened and was nearly swollen shut.

God, I looked terrible!

Avan dampened a washcloth. The closed lid creaked as he sat and began dabbing gently at the cut on my cheek.

"How's your hand?" I asked after a long silence.

He smiled a small smile, shifted the cloth to his right hand, and flexed the fingers of his left. It was wet, the blood washed away, his knuckles swollen.

"It still works," he said pleasantly, ignoring the noticeable bruising.

It was adrenaline. It had to be. When it burned off, when he exhausted it, when he came down from the high of the fight? He'd collapse. I had to be strong, push past my pain, and convince him I was alright. Only then might I get him to rest before he dropped.

"And your mouth?" I asked, staring at the flakes of blood in his goatee.

Avan felt the back of his mouth with his tongue. When he did, I realized he'd had no mouth guard. He shrugged his shoulders, unfazed.

"Tooth must've caught my cheek when he hit me. It's just a little cut. The face has hundreds of blood vessels, remember?"

I swallowed, remembering a particularly nauseating cage fight where Avan's opponent cut his forehead after Avan delivered a powerful high kick. Nausea roiled my stomach as the blood gushed from his head, blinding him, spilling into his nose and mouth. Yet when his face was wiped clean, there was only a tiny cut in the center of his forehead. The wound that seemed so horrific was little more than a large paper cut.

There was no point in asking Avan about the rest of his body, so I sat and let him dab lightly at my cheek with the cloth. My eyes fluttered from his face to his free hand that I so desperately wanted to hold. Through his fingers, I saw his shin, black and blue like his ribs, and I asked him the same question I always did.

"Doesn't that hurt?"

He jerked his head in negation. "The hits hurt more when you're not expecting them."

In my head, I replayed his beating, Kaine and the others throwing the hood over Avan's head and hitting him with everything they had, every blow unexpected. If what he said was true, then it must have been agony.

I inhaled a shaky breath. Avan's hand pulled back, his brow furrowed.

"Am I hurting you?"

The basement door creaked open before I could shake my head. Heavy boots descended and when our captor stood in the doorway of the bathroom, I didn't react. I felt safer with Avan between me and him, though my cowardice shamed me. Avan's dark eyebrows drew closer together as he watched our captor set an ice pack and water bottle on the counter next to the sink. Taking a step further into the room, Kaine roughly patted Avan on the back. I didn't like it but held my tongue.

"You put up a good fight tonight, Gutierrez."

Everything inside me blazed. Touching me was one thing. Laying his filthy hands on Avan was another.

It spoke to the power he already held over us that, even with no knife in his hand, neither Avan nor I attempted to escape. We knew the others were upstairs, waiting for us with zip-ties and hoods and who knew what else. We couldn't see them, but we knew they were up there.

"Four days to recover," Kaine said, taking a bottle of anti-inflammatories from his coat pocket. "That's it. Then you fight again."

He set the bottle on top of the ice pack. It rolled onto the floor, its lid staying firmly closed, but my mind was on what he said.

Four days? Four days until the next three rounds of fighting?

Avan always needed several weeks, sometimes a few months, to recover when he fought professionally. He had a team of nurses and doctors on call whenever he needed them. But here? What if he broke something? What if he was hit so hard that he didn't wake up?

"Four days?!" I snapped, standing up. "Four fucking days? That's not long enough!"

Avan grabbed my wrist, and it burned my skin. I glanced at him, then watched our captor go, grinning at my anger before walking up the stairs and out the door. My chest heaved. I clenched my fists.

"Hey," Avan said, pulling me down. "Hey, it's okay. Sit down."

I thumped onto the tub, feeling the weight of the world beginning to crash down on my shoulders. Avan took my hands. My tears were hot.

"Don't do this, Avan," I begged. "Please, don't do this."

He squeezed my fingers. "It'll be okay," he said, a little softer now. "I'll be okay. I'll get us out of here. I promise."

"Four days, Avan," I whispered through clenched teeth. "That's all you get. Look at you!" I gestured to his body.

He placed his hands on either side of my neck, his thumbs brushing my jawline. He spoke so softly I could hardly hear him. "I can handle it. I have to."

My chest tightened, constricting on my words, holding them in, but I spoke up anyway.

"But what if you can't? What if you tear something or break something? What if you get hit so hard you-"

I didn't finish. I couldn't finish. I couldn't breathe. Avan was talking to me, his words muffled, his voice too quiet to be heard. His face swam in and out of focus. My hands found his elbows. I knew I was squeezing them, hurting him, but my thoughts were spinning, my mind unable to control my body.

"I'm here," a muffled voice said. "Focus on me. That's It. Just focus on me. I'm right here with you..."

AVAN SAT BESIDE ME on the couch and passed me a glass of water. "Feeling any better?"

The water shook in my hands as I took a sip and set it on the coffee table. I sighed, slouching into the cushions. God, I was exhausted.

Avan turned to face me, his elbow against the back. I closed my eyes, not answering him. For a long time, we sat like that, me trying to get a grip on my thoughts, him brushing the hair out of my face. My breathing slowed to match his and I remembered seeing him, a blurry silhouette in the height of my panic, breathing slowly, deeply, until I did the same. Until I calmed down. I opened my eyes, not looking at him.

"How do you know so much about anxiety attacks?"

"I don't."

I lifted my head from the pillows and looked at him. "What?"

He smirked. "Do you know what makes our strikes so powerful? How we feel next to nothing when we get hit?"

I knew who he was talking about, but wasn't sure how it applied to my anxiety. This was a question that wasn't meant to be answered. So, I stayed quiet until he answered it himself.

"Breathing."

I raised an eyebrow and he grinned.

"We breathe with each strike."

He sat up and demonstrated, closing his fists. As he punched at the air, he exhaled, fast and loud, through clenched teeth.

"It's all about control." he continued, sitting back and leaning towards me. "If you can't control your breathing when someone is

swinging at you and vice-versa, what can you control? Breathing is key."

He kissed my hair and got up, taking the blanket from the back of the couch. I smiled and lay down. He draped the blanket over me and tucked it in, leaning close.

"Sleep," he whispered in my ear.

He kissed me again, on my cheek, then very carefully placed his hand over my eyes, closing them for me. Though my eyes were closed, I still felt him crouching down In front of me. He ran his hand through my hair, leaving me feeling something I'd never felt before: peace.

"BABY, CAN YOU HEAR me?"

I could. Avan's face came into focus, his breathing slow and steady, like mine. My hands slipped off his arms, too clammy to gain traction, but I could breathe again.

"You're okay." Avan soothed. "I've got you. Everything is okay."

But everything wasn't okay. I didn't look at him. I slid off the side of the tub and fell into his arms. After all, it was the safest place I could be.

Chapter Nine

The basement was cozy but disorienting. The only light we had was from dim lamps on the end tables set on either side of the bed. There was no clock, and with no windows, no natural light? Time was unknowable.

Even after Avan assured me he'd be fine to stay awake and keep watch, claiming his adrenaline spike would keep him up for most of the night anyway, I was the restless one. I couldn't stop thinking, worrying about what was to come. Neither of us slept.

After hours of tossing and turning, I finally had enough. I needed to get up, move around, do something. I woke Avan and brought him to the bathroom. I remembered he had cleaned my wound, but I had neglected to tend to him. The water bottle was still there. So was the ice pack, partially melted but usable, and the bottle of painkillers.

He sat on the edge of the tub while I sat on the closed lid of the toilet, a damp washcloth in my hand, eager to take care of him, to put my mind at ease.

"Tell me if I hurt you."

Avan inhaled through his nose, smiling as he did. "You're too gentle to hurt me." he soothed.

His smile grew sweeter, as if his cuts and bruises didn't affect him. In the bright light of the bathroom, I could see them more clearly: the swelling below his eye, the cuts on his cheeks, the bruises to his upper body. As much as I hated watching the fights that left him this way, I loved caring for him. I loved seeing the relief on his face, the knowledge I was dulling his pain, if only for a moment. I loved feeling wanted, needed, treasured.

His eyes followed my hand as I wiped away the blood. Rubbing alcohol was the only disinfectant in the cabinet under the sink. I took it out and poured it onto the washcloth.

"This'll probably hurt like Hell."

Avan shrugged and half-smiled. "Nothing I can't handle."

I sucked in my breath and dabbed at the cuts on his face. He winced and pulled back, sucking in a sharp breath.

"Easy!"

I jerked my hand back, anxiety pricking through me.

"I'm sorry!" My heart raced at the edge of panic.

He laughed lightly and grinned. "I'm kidding. It's not that bad."

I glowered at him. "I hate you!" But there was no heat in my words.

He puckered his lips, yearning for a kiss. I dabbed carefully at the wound beneath his eye instead. He winced a little, then frowned, sensing my lingering anxiety.

"You're doing great." His words were intentionally playful. "You deserve a billion dollars and a pony."

I blushed. I brushed my hair behind my ear with my free hand. Though I didn't need to, the action was the only thing keeping me from giggling like a silly, love-crazed schoolgirl.

I took the ice from the counter and placed it on the dark patch of bruises on his ribcage. He flinched. After a few seconds he cried out, so loud I jumped. Then I laughed. I laughed, because he laughed, the small joyous sound flowing easily from his mouth. I shoved him playfully, just hard enough to make his fingers grip the edge of the tub a little tighter.

"You're a jackass!"

He grinned again. "There's the beautiful smile I was looking for."

My cheeks flushed, and as easily as that, my cautiousness and fear melted away. He was always doing it, lightening my mood with a joke or two, a playful jab at my expense like my brother used to do.

He didn't flinch when I put the pack onto his lower chest, just stared at me with the sweetest of smiles. He sighed, relief plain on his face.

"Thank you."

I reached for the painkillers. Avan told me that bruised ribs were the most painful. They were the only injury he openly complained about. Unthinking, I handed them to him, thinking he'd open the lid with no trouble at all. When he tried, twisting the lid with his left hand and holding the bottle in his right, he cursed under his breath and gave his wrist a quick flick in irritation. I placed my hand on the lid of the bottle and opened it.

He popped two pills into his mouth and took a few gulps from the water bottle. After I'd set the bottles on the counter, he leaned forward and kissed me. His lips were cold, mouth tempting. He lingered close enough I could feel the warmth of his breath on my lips, long enough I could feel him waiting for me to kiss him back. I did, taking his face in my hands, pressing my lips firmly against his, my mouth hungry for more. It felt like forever since we'd kissed like this, full of passion and depth. Stolen breaths.

It didn't last long.

Avan pulled back and clapped a hand to his side. I looked down and realized I'd dropped the pack of ice. He sighed angrily, frustrated by his injuries. I ignored the ice and touched his jaw with the barest brush of my fingertips. Tears wedged themselves into the corners of my eyes. I couldn't kiss him without hurting him. He lifted his gaze to meet mine and placed his hands on either side of my neck, his green eyes catching and holding me.

"I can do this," he whispered.

I felt the urge to pull back, startled by this random change of topic, but then Avan pressed his lips against my forehead, grounding me, steadying me, preventing my total collapse. I never wanted to lose this sense of safety, this sense of peace that he always seemed to bring whenever he was near. I couldn't live without this, without him. I had to get him out of this death trap. I had to fight for him before these fights took him from me forever.

I COULD STILL FEEL Avan's mouth on my body, his hands searching for worlds unknown, fingers discovering buried treasures, green eyes seeking parts of me that he had yet to touch. I shivered as we lay in our bed, our bare legs tangled in blankets and bedsheets, our naked bodies so close that I felt as though we were zipped in the same skin. As always, it was Avan who broke the silence.

"*Can I ask you something?*" *His thumb brushed my shoulder, and his skin tightened as my fingers drew circles along his flat stomach.*

"*Always.*" *I replied.*

He let out a soft sound of pleasure, then continued. "Do you remember when I told you that I was a professional fighter? I asked if it bothered you and you looked at me. You never said anything, but while we were having sex, you seemed sort of cautious. Like you were afraid you were going to hurt me or something."

He was right. I hadn't touched him like I usually did when we made love. My hands hadn't gripped his elbows or pressed down on his chest or pulled on his shoulders. My fingers hadn't even tugged lightly at his hair. I swallowed. Hurt colored my cheeks. I'd acted like I didn't want him, like I hadn't felt the same ecstasy that I always felt when he centered himself on top of me. I swallowed again.

"*You said you were sore, didn't you?*"

His shoulders lifted. "I can handle a bit of soreness. It's part of my job, you know?"

I didn't say anything. I didn't want to say anything. What could I tell him that he hadn't heard millions of times before? And why was he still asking about it?

"*You don't have to hold anything back from me," Avan said as if reading my thoughts. "Ever." He paused. "I just wonder... Why do you stay with me when it bothers you so much?*"

I touched my fingers to his collarbone. "Because of what you did. In your last fight."

Avan's eyebrows drew closer to each other as he looked at my face. "What did I do?"

My hand slid down to his chest. I closed my eyes, remembering one of the few times I felt good about watching the fights.

"You didn't go for the kick." I felt him staring at me, waiting for me to continue. "You didn't kick him as he went down. You helped him regain consciousness, I mean, you helped him stand up. You even kissed him on the cheek when he hugged you. You respected him and he respected you."

I opened my eyes, looking up at him. He was smiling now. I laughed as I admitted, "Honestly, I always thought MMA fighters were complete assholes."

Avan laughed. "Some of us are."

I pressed a finger into his chest. "You're not."

He stayed silent, his smile fading. I ran my fingernails slowly up and down the length of his arm. He shivered.

"You're kind, thoughtful, compassionate. You care about people, like really care about them."

His chest rose and fell. "I could be better."

He was always doing that, discounting my praise, never seeming to believe my compliments.

"You have a good heart, Avan. Why is that so hard to believe?"

His body tensed. His eyes turned away from me. That's when it happened again. He was in another world. I saw pain on his face and I suddenly wanted to make up for not touching him the way he craved. He was quiet for a long moment before speaking with a broken voice.

"Y-you don't know everything about me. There's awful stuff you don't know about me, stuff I- I wish I could take back."

I wasn't ready to talk about this. No matter what he'd done, he had changed. I could see it in his interactions with other fighters. I saw it in the way he crouched in front of them to wipe at their tears after they'd lost, the way he took them into his arms, the way he raised their arm in victory even when he'd won.

"You're not that person anymore." I said quickly. "I know you're not."

Avan gulped down his sadness. He inhaled a slow trembling breath. "I don't know about that."

I didn't want to hear anymore. I sat up and pressed my mouth to his. I heard him choke back a sob, felt his brow furrowed as he frowned, but his arms encircled me, his strong hands pressed against my shoulder blades. Something wet hit my cheek—a tear. But I wasn't the one crying.

I kissed him fiercely, my breath huffing into his mouth, my arms trapping. And, I had him. He rolled over, taking me with him, and pushed me into the mattress. I gripped his elbows. His sudden intake of breath told me everything I needed to know. I ran my fingers down his arms and made him focus on me.

I OPENED MY EYES, SLEEPY and disoriented. Avan had fallen asleep with his arm over me, his face buried in my hair, his breath hot on the nape of my neck. I still had his fingers tangled in mine.

God, it was freezing!

I carefully pulled the blanket up over us, wanting to not disturb Avan. Too late. I felt him stir as he awoke, his fingers twitching against mine. He drew a long, tired breath, moving slightly away from me. I turned to face him. He muttered an apology, rubbing a hand over the side of his face and trying to wake himself up. It hit me that he was always apologizing, always blaming himself, even when he'd done nothing wrong. Like now.

"I'll keep watch," I whispered. "Go back to sleep."

I knew he wouldn't. Avan pushed himself hard. He didn't, or couldn't, sleep after he awoke in the dead of night. He slept for no more than three or four hours a night. Most nights, it was racing thoughts and anxieties he rarely shared with me and kept him from the bed. Other nights, it was nightmares that left him too terrified to fall back to sleep. Tonight, I knew exactly what it was that was keeping him awake.

"I can take care of myself, ya know?" I teased, forcing a smirk.

"I know you can." His voice was too serious. He placed his thumb beneath the cut on my cheek. I winced, feeling the sting of it. "But I'm not taking any chances. If you got hurt again. If they ra-"

He stopped. He lowered his eyes. I knew what he'd been about to say. When I looked back on the kidnapping cases I'd seen on television through the years, when I remembered the horrific stories told by female victims, I caught myself. When I remembered what Kaine had said, what he threatened to do to me, I caught myself again. I couldn't argue with Avan. His concern for my safety was justified.

Avan's voice conveyed the emotions he was trying to hide. His words trembled with the tears he refused to show. "I couldn't forgive myself if anything happened to you. If I let something happen to you. I'd rather... I'd rather suffer than watch you hurt."

I looked at him with admiring eyes and I brushed away a few strands of hair from his cheek. My words came out sharper than I'd intended. "You need to rest, Avan."

His lips set in a hard line, and his gaze became deep. "I'll never let them hurt you. I'll keep you safe."

I shuddered. I wanted to change the subject, to do something to distract him and myself from our circumstances. My mind drew a blank. I thought hard for a moment about what we could possibly do in a small room with nothing but a bed and a bathroom. Then, it hit me: the perfect distraction.

"Do you remember," I began, holding the ends of his hair between my fingertips. "That game we used to play when I'd come to stay with you in the hospital?"

He smiled and answered by playing it. "What if we get out of here? What if I win every fight that's thrown at me? What if we were lying in our bed right now?"

My heart raced. I don't know how I dared to add my next words, but I did.

"What if... What if, one day, we woke up to the pitter-patter of little feet on the floor?"

Avan's eyes grew soft, their green forests damp with the possibility. He played his next words slowly. "What if I got down on one knee," He took me by the hand. He laced his fingers in with mine. "And promised you the world?"

I blinked very, very slowly. Did he mean it? When I looked into his eyes, into his growing smile, I knew he did.

"Yes," I breathed, smiling wildly. "Yes, Avan. Yes!"

He chuckled, sporting the same stupid grin, and he wrapped his arms around me. For the briefest of moments, our wounds didn't touch us. We weren't in the basement anymore.

And we weren't being held captive by a sadistic monster. We were two souls in one body, zipped up in the same skin.

Chapter Ten

Our peace was broken by muffled shouting, glass shattering, and a door slamming. When the basement door opened, Avan and I were on our feet.

"Stay behind me." Avan ordered.

I retreated, my eyes peeking over his shoulder. Kaine held something made from a thin flexible material - bamboo. It seemed familiar, and I puzzled over it for a moment until my mind dredged up the memory. It looked identical to the canes used to lash the secular blogger Raif Badawi in Saudi Arabia. It was a cane built for beating prisoners and slaves. In the other hand, he held the knife.

Kaine gestured towards the floor with the cane.

"Lay down."

We hesitated.

"Get down, dog!"

I jumped. Avan obeyed, and I started down.

"Not you," said Kaine, looking at me.

Avan lay with his chest against the floor, his hands braced as if preparing to do a push-up. A cruel smile spread across Ksine's face. He was pleased, and I was frightened for Avan.

"Get on his back." He gestured towards me with the knife.

I did. Avan lifted himself enough for me to wrap my arms around his chest, underneath his pectoral muscles, my cheek resting on his shoulder. I felt him raise his head, no doubt looking up at Kaine and his henchmen. I didn't look.

"Push-ups," Kaine said. "Until I say stop."

Avan inhaled as he rose, his sharp shoulder blade becoming smooth, then exhaled, lowering us to the floor. I felt a sudden rush of affection toward him, a closeness that grew as he repeated the action over and over. He wasn't only carrying himself. He was carrying me as he always had.

His breathing was rhythmic and controlled, like he did during my many anxiety attacks. His back supported me even with the weight of the world on his shoulders. I never loved someone so deeply in my entire life.

I squeezed my arms tighter around him. I pressed my cheek into his shoulder and closed my eyes, soaking in the soothing heat radiating from his back, his chest, his legs. If I didn't let him go, I'd be alright.

"HEY, SHORT STUFF!"

I climbed out of bed and followed the sound of my brother's voice to the living room. He looked at me, his pale eyes welcoming. I smiled at him, a scrawny child still in her pajamas.

"Wanna help me work out?" he asked, getting up from the couch.

I giggled. I was too small to be a spotter, and all his weights were in the garage.

"How?"

He lay on the carpet with his chest against the floor.

"Climb on," he said.

I took a few steps towards him. "On your back?"

He smiled. "Are ya scared?" He didn't say it meanly, more as a challenge, so I shot him a dark look and climbed on, my little arms around his neck. He pushed off the ground so fast that I bounced against him, giggling and laughing.

"Better hold on!" he said.

I squeezed him tighter. He went down fast. My stomach rose and fell, making me laugh again. He repeated the action once, twice, three times before finally slowing to a regular pace. I closed my eyes, full of joy at seeing him before football season started up again. I didn't want him to leave.

After about twenty push-ups, my brother's body stilled, waiting for me to get off. But I didn't want to. I held on. And nothing in the world would have encouraged me to let go.

I MISSED MY BROTHER. I missed the way he smelled. I missed his laugh, his smile, his hugs. I missed the way he teased and tricked me even in my teens. That was before the concussions, before his hallucinations, before he started hearing voices, before I found him hanging from the beam in our basement.

Avan grunted as he lowered us slowly to the floor. His breathing, so steady before, had grown rapid and choppy. A musky smell hit my nostrils. He was sweating so heavily my shirt was soaked with it. I could feel his heart pounding above my hands. His limbs trembled beneath me. He was exhausted.

How many push-ups had he done? Sixty? Seventy? More?

"Off!" Kaine ordered.

Avan and I flinched. Before I could respond, Kaine grabbed me. He pulled me off, dragging me so hard that my knees gave way. He pushed me into the arms of the other men.

Avan shouted as he rose, "Get your hands off her!"

Kaine turned and kicked Avan in his already injured ribs, forcing him onto the ground. My arms were pinned behind my back as I tried to get away. Kaine stood over Avan with the cane, staring down at him.

"Did I tell you to stop?"

Avan said nothing. He looked up at Kaine, holding his side and breathing hard through the pain and exhaustion. He looked past Kaine towards me, his expression frightened.

"She won't be touched," Kaine assured. "As long as you comply." His voice was smooth, like a used car salesman. He waited a moment, then said quickly, "Push-ups."

For the second time, Avan obeyed. He assumed his position, resting his chest against the floor, and pushed himself up.

A sickening *crack* rang out, wood on bone, the cane contacting Avan's shoulder. I cringed. Avan collapsed, his teeth gritted, his cheek against the smooth wood floor. As he lay there, his rapid breaths fogging the floor's shiny surface, I thought about all the times I'd buried my face into that shoulder. I remembered every time Avan pulled me close, soothing me, comforting me as he always did. The soft, unblemished skin was sliced through with a bleeding welt. Determination battled with pain in my chest.

"No!" I snapped. "Stop!"

The men held me as I fought to get to Avan, their fingers pinching the skin of my arms. Kaine bent down and shouted his command in Avan's ear.

"Push-ups!"

Slowly, Avan rose, his shoulders shaking.

Crack!

With a grunt, he fell back onto the floor, his eyes squeezed firmly shut. I couldn't watch this anymore. I fought harder until I was forced down onto my knees.

"Come on, Gutierrez." Kaine taunted, walking to Avan's other side. "You don't want your little girlfriend getting hurt now, do you?"

Avan opened his eyes. For a moment, we looked at each other. We saw the suffering in one another's eyes. Avan pressed his lips together. His expression became rigid. He turned his face ahead of him, his hair falling over his eyes, and rose with a sharp intake of breath.

"Avan, stay down!"

Crack!

Avan gasped, his leg giving out. He lifted his head, his face downcast, and rose again.

Crack!

Avan stayed down. He rolled onto his side, green eyes finding me.

"Avan," I mouthed. "Please."

I knew he would go on. I could see it in his face, his determination pushing away the pain. I knew he would go however far Kaine pushed. He would endure so I wouldn't face Kaine's wrath. His entire frame was shaking now.

"You see gentlemen," Kaine said, looking towards me and the men. "This man is no stranger to pain."

He tapped the end of the cane to Avan's shoulder. Then he looked at me, his gaze dark and slow.

"And neither am I."

The fifth blow was the loudest, the sharp sound echoing off the basement walls. It was that blow that kept Avan on the ground. I gasped, feeling relieved and horrified, when it was clear he wouldn't be rising again.

Kaine dragged the stick across the hardwood floor. He motioned to the men, and all four of them went up the stairs, locking the door.

"Avan," I said, kneeling beside him. "Avan, what can I do?"

He opened his eyes, his face painted with worry at the sight of my expression. With a wince, he rose up onto his elbows, raising one knee. His breathing was hard and uneven.

"Are you okay?" I asked, taking his hand.

He wasn't. He swallowed hard and smiled faintly. That smile washed away my pain, my grief, my anguish.

"No sweat, babe."

Despite the obvious weakness to his voice, I chose to believe him. My fingers squeezed his as I helped him sit the rest of the way up.

THE SWELLING IN HIS cheek was gone, leaving a dark yellowish bruise in its wake. This was a good thing. Avan was healing.

I rubbed Avan's back the night before his next fight, kneeling behind him when he sat down on the end of the bed. His hair was still wet from his shower, and his skin was damp. I felt it as I ran my hands up the length of his back, my palms gentle.

"Like I showed you." Avan reminded.

I inhaled, my hands stopping. His back was painted with new and old wounds. Misshapen bruises rose under his skin. Rough scabs formed where fresh cuts once bled. The strokes of the cane, long red marks across his shoulders and back, were too painful to look at.

"You're sure?" I asked, nervous.

He nodded, his head low.

I pressed my palms into his skin. Immediately, I felt the knots, the countless tight muscles, the spongey, blood-filled bruises. I hesitated for a moment, then pushed harder. Already, I felt the knot under my thumbs starting to loosen. Avan groaned. He moaned softly, his skin quivering. The muscles twitched.

"Does that hurt?"

He shook his head. "Keep going."

I kept rubbing out his knots and pushing the pockets of blood away from the worst of his bruises. Just yesterday, I'd watched him rub the bruises out of his shin, an excruciatingly painful process for every fighter, no matter how experienced.

He saw me looking from where he sat at the edge of the bed and smiled. "It's all part of it, babe. You know that."

I sat back against the wall behind me, remembering one of the few times I'd ever seen Avan cry. We were at the gym for what Avan playfully called his "rub-out session." Avan would sit on a mat, his leg stretched in front of him as Jeff, his sparring partner, gently rubbed his shin with a blissfully scented oil. Once Jeff had rubbed in the lubricant, he used his thumbs to slowly push the blood upward, pressing as hard as he dared. I remembered Avan's screams, muffled by the towel, tears pooling in his eyes. Despite my constant worries and anxieties, I couldn't hold back my laughter. Here was Avan, so strong, so tough, so unbreakable, crying as Jeff told him to think of sunshine and rainbows. I teased him afterward, and we'd spent the rest of that day poking fun at each other, debating on who was the bigger wimp.

Avan sharply sucked in his breath as he ran his thumbs firmly over the skin closest to the bone. I looked away.

"How can you stand it?" I asked.

"Like I said," he began, voice strangled as he rubbed out another bruise. "Pain is a part of it. It's how you deal with the pain that matters. If you control it, it won't control you."

As I sat behind him on the bed now, he leaned forward and rested his mouth against his clasped hands. His shoulders shuddered under my fingers. Although I couldn't see them, I knew his eyes were closed.

"What are you thinking?" I asked, curling my fingers around his ears and neck.

When he didn't say anything, I let my fingers slide down to his shoulders and gave them a gentle squeeze. This caught his attention. His words were soft. "Did you mean it?"

Now it was my turn to stay quiet. I stayed like that for so long that Avan spoke before I responded.

"When you said you wanted to have children with me."

I moved the wet strands of hair behind his ear, and leaned my chin on his shoulder, my smooth cheek against his stubbled one. I wrapped my arms around his neck.

"Of course I did," I whispered.

I felt his fingers wrap around my wrist. "Why?"

I repositioned my legs and leaned back, taking him with me. We fell onto the soft blanket behind us. I kept my voice gentle.

"Why is it so hard to believe that someone could love you, Avan?"

Avan stayed quiet. I hated these new-found moments of thoughtfulness he seemed to fall into. Why did he need to think so hard about this? I was suddenly furious with him, but now was not the time to show it. He had enough to worry about. I swallowed my anger.

"Go to sleep," I whispered.

He turned his head onto my breast and closed his eyes. After several minutes, his fingers twitched against my palm, his breathing deepened, and his muscles relaxed. I sighed. He was finally asleep. I watched him, my fingers drawing pointless patterns across the bridge of his nose, the line of his jaw, the curve of his ear. He snored softly, and I giggled at the sound.

His lips parted ever so slightly to expose his teeth, stained by time and coffee, a little chipped from a cage fight that ended with his opponent hitting him hard enough to send his mouthguard flying out of the octagon.

I traced his eyebrows. I played with his hair. I watched him sleep through it all. His features, so delicate, seemed even more precious when I thought of our circumstances. His next fight was tomorrow and we had no idea who his opponent would be.

A strong jab could fracture a cheekbone, knock out a tooth, or shatter an eye socket. A kick could do even worse.

Not for the first time, it struck me that MMA fighters were like modern day gladiators, and Avan was one of them. He was skilled and he was strong.

But would strength and skill be enough to win?

Chapter Eleven

Avan kissed me before heading into the octagon, his lips dry and tense. I couldn't remember the last time he'd had a drink, so I picked up the water bottle Kaine had given us.

"Avan!" I called over the roaring crowd.

Avan took the bottle from my hand and tipped it back, his cheeks swelling with water. He spat out most and swallowed what little was left.

I remembered something he'd said once and understood. "Ever been punched in the gut with a stomach full of water?" I winced at the memory, my hand on my empty stomach. Avan was already in the cage before he could see. The door was locked. The fight was on.

Avan's opponent was thin and lanky, much like him. *This is a good thing*, I thought

As soon as the fight started, I knew I was wrong.

Avan was slow. His strikes were weak. He stumbled getting up after being taken down.

As if on cue, my stomach ached and rumbled audibly. Neither Avan nor I had eaten in more than a week. As if realizing the situation, my body rebelled. I felt how weak I'd become, how my knees trembled under my weight, how my body seemed enveloped with fatigue. I was dizzy and nauseous, and I was just standing.

Avan was in constant motion, exerting what energy he had left. He wouldn't last much longer. Soon, he wouldn't be able to fight. Avan's will was strong, but starvation was stronger. Low blood sugar didn't care about will. Hunger and weakness would ultimately bring him down. I swallowed a hungry breath and watched Avan carefully.

He was down, his legs wrapped around his opponent. His skin was already dripping with sweat, despite being only minutes into the first round. I wrung my hands. My palms were slippery and clammy. I watched Avan take repeated punches to his head, his face. His nose bled.

"Get up, Avan!" I yelled.

He didn't hear me, the crowd too loud. He stayed there, on the ground, and took the beating. Blood was smeared all over his face, his opponent's fists slipping in the mess of red that streamed from Avan's nose and mouth.

"Come on, Avan," I whispered, clasping my hands. "What are you doing?"

Finally, Avan locked his arms around his opponent's neck and head. He twisted his body and brought the guy down onto his back. In seconds, they'd traded positions, Avan on top, punching as hard as he could, and his opponent struggling helplessly beneath him. Minutes later, Avan had the man in a chokehold and the man tapped out.

The second round was a flurry of fists and blood. It ended quickly. Avan was knocked down again, his opponent trapping him in an ankle lock. Unable to break free, Avan held out as long as he could, gritting his teeth and burying his face into the canvas as if it were sand. When he finally tapped out, his ankle had been twisted to the point where I was sure something had torn or broken.

By the start of the third round, he was limping. Within seconds, he was on his back again. He kicked his opponent off him and rose on unsteady legs. He swayed on his feet and fell forward, dizzy and disoriented. He stayed where he was, on his hands and knees, and let his opponent bring him down once more. After several punches, his opponent backed off.

Avan got up, steadying himself by grabbing the cage behind him. He panted, exhausted, desperate, defeated. His eyebrows loomed over his eyes. His stance changed, his left hip back. His eyes narrowed onto his opponent. The young man was distracted, looking into the crowd, gloating instead of staying focused. He was an amateur. Avan let go of the cage, swaying, before delivering his final blow: a kick to the head.

His opponent fell like he'd been shot. He didn't get up. I rushed to the cage door, cheering, but Avan was distracted, watching with worried eyes. He crouched to lift the man's legs as Kaine pushed past me and unlocked the cage.

"He's not waking up!" Avan said.

Kaine grabbed Avan by the arm and the sheer brutality made my blood run hot.

"Let's go, Gutierrez!"

Kaine forced Avan to his feet and pulled him out of the octagon. As they went down the stairs, Avan looked over his shoulder. The man still hadn't moved. I heard Avan draw in his breath.

"No... No!"

He fought against Kaine, squirming out of his grasp, and leaped onto the cage, climbing over the edge and falling back into the ring.

Two men rushed past me, opened the door to the cage, and grabbed Avan, Kaine following close behind. He tried fighting them off, but the last bit of adrenaline, the surge that got him up and over the cage, had run its course.

Another man held me back, pinning my arms. The way Avan peered at Kaine through his tousled hair was eerie, his shoulders low, his knees bent, his face bloodied. This was more than exhaustion that consumed him. This was pure anger. His flat tone made the hair on my arms stand at attention.

"I'm not leaving until he wakes up."

Kaine stared him, stared until I was sure I could feel Avan seething with rage.

"Fine!" He looked towards me and snapped his fingers. For a second, I didn't know what he wanted. I saw the water bottle and made the connection. I stumbled into the cage and Kaine took the bottle from my hands. He walked to where the young man lay and poured the water over the man's face until he coughed and came to.

"Happy?" Kaine threw the half-empty bottle to the floor and gestured for the men to let Avan go. I didn't need to wonder why no one in the crowd was stopping this madness. They were here for the drama.

When the men released him, Avan slumped to the floor. He covered his eyes and curled forward, his head on his knees.

AVAN LIMPED TO THE bathroom as soon as we entered the basement. He ran the sink and splashed cold water onto his hair and face. When he came out, the blood was gone.

He fell onto the bed with a groan. I sat beside him, trying desperately to make sense of his reaction. He shivered from the cold, so I took off my jacket. I walked to his side of the bed and asked him to sit up. He did, sitting cross-legged on the bed as I wrapped my coat around him. He thanked me quietly and said nothing more, tightening the jacket around himself. The silence stretched until I couldn't stand it any longer.

"What happened back there?"

"Don't worry about it," he said. He sounded flustered, like my question annoyed him. He shuddered again, closing his eyes and lowering his head. His teeth chattered.

"I've just never seen you... freak out like that before."

He made a noise, caught between a sigh and a groan. and repositioned himself on the bed, stretching out and lying down. "I won," he said. "Isn't that what matters?"

He wasn't saying anything more, and I didn't want to fight with him. Not now, not in this situation.

I reached for his swollen ankle. He jerked his foot away. I grunted softly and tried to smooth the edge of iron out of my words. "Just let me see."

He kept his knee bent.

"Avan, I'm trying to help. If we talked about what happened, I could-"

He grabbed at his hair and snapped at me. "Just drop it!"

I flinched. Avan had never raised his voice to me before. After a few moments of silence, he looked guiltily at me. His voice was softer now, gentler, though the sharpness was still there.

"Just leave it alone, please. I'm exhausted."

He rolled away from me, his head on his arm. I lay beside him and rubbed his shoulder. His muscles, his whole body, tensed at my touch.

He sniffed. He was crying, or at least, close to crying, because his nose was runny. I could hear it. I turned over and rested my head against the pillow. In my head, the incident replayed: Avan leaping onto the cage, sinking to the floor, curling in defeat. But he had won. It didn't make sense.

I shook my head, too tired, too confused to make sense of it now. Instead, I reached a hand behind me. My fingers rested on Avan's hip. After a while, I felt his hand. His fingers closed around mine. His grip was slack, evidence of his anger, but it was enough. Even he knew this wasn't the time to be distant. We were all we had in this crazy, terrible, fucked-up new life of ours.

Chapter Twelve

I remembered the expression on Avan's face when I asked about his scars.

We were standing in the locker room minutes before a fight, doing breathing exercises with his eyes closed as I wrapped his hands and wrists with thin white tape and a strip of cotton cloth. As I placed his thumb through the loop at the end of the cloth, I noticed a large dark reddish-brown circle, a burn scar, on the skin between his thumb and index finger. I held the wrap with one hand and took Avan's fingers in the other, touching the scar.

"What happened here?"

He opened his eyes, his face in a slight frown as he gently pulled his hand away. The fingers of his other hand touched the scar, his thumb rubbing it slowly. His voice was thoughtful; thoughtful and soft, as it always was.

"I didn't exactly have the nicest foster parents in the world."

I shivered, remembering what he told me about his time in Foster Care, how much harder life was. But he was hesitant and hadn't gone into much detail. I shuddered again when I realized what he meant.

I'd seen scars like this before. I'd seen them when we made love. I'd seen them when he changed his clothes in front of me. I'd seen them when I joined him in the bath or shower. They were scattered across the back of his hands, the inside of his wrists, the tender skin above his ankles. They were even on his belly. I'd never asked him about any of them until now.

"Avan..." I whispered.

I didn't know what I had been planning to say. I lifted my hand to his hair, and let my fingers slide from the long thick strands to his cheek. He leaned into my hand for a moment and blinked.

He smiled at me, a beautiful, reassuring grin, and rested his hand on top of mine. He pulled my fingers away from his face and kissed them, our mutual expression of love, of comfort, of thanks. His eyes stared into mine and I felt my sorrow fade away. He kissed me and I wrapped his hands, my eyes avoiding his scars, my thoughts drifting toward the fight ahead.

I came back from the memory. Here we were, trying to sleep in a bed that wasn't ours. Avan had rolled over and was sleeping with his hand on my shoulder, his chest pressed against my back, his breath hot in my ear.

Faintly, I felt the beat of his heart. I felt his breathing, slow and calm. I felt the faint twitch of his fingers, and exhaled. He was completely at peace, unconcerned. My thoughts drifted to the fights ahead, the fights that promised freedom.

Risk wasn't a promise. It was guaranteed. Avan and every other fighter risked their lives, their safety, their bodies, every time they stepped into the cage. The stakes were higher now. Avan wasn't fighting for the glory anymore. He was fighting for our lives.

Chapter Thirteen

It happened in the final round, the thing I'd been dreading since this nightmare began.

Avan was lifted into the air and slammed onto the canvas.

It had been my worst fear since Avan told me he fought for a living.

His head thudded, loud and distinct, onto the rough material of the canvas.

It had been my worst fear since I watched my brother lifted onto a stretcher after a bad tackle in his final football game.

His eyes closed and he didn't get up.

I could feel Avan's lips on my forehead. I could feel his hands cradling my face, and hear the words, "I will win."

I felt it all over again as I watched him go down, his head bouncing against the canvas. He lay perfectly still.

I yelled his name.

He didn't wake up.

"PUT THE GUN DOWN, GABE," I whispered.

He stood by the kitchen counter, holding our father's gun in his hand.

"Gabriel," I said, stepping closer to him. "Give me the gun."

He looked at me, his tear-stained face echoing months of depression.

"I need it to stop!"

I flinched at his tone.

"You need what to stop?"

He buried his head into his hands.

"The voices," he sobbed. "I can't- I need them to stop!"

He was yelling now, furious, devastated, terrified. I swallowed. Gabe wasn't afraid of anything. It was always him who chased away my fears. He was the strongest person I knew, the one who'd held me as a baby, the boy I idolized and looked up to since I was born. This Gabriel? This wasn't my brother anymore.

"It'll be okay, Gabe." I assured. "Maybe the doctor can h-"

He interrupted me, his voice full of his tears. "He can't help me. No one can help me!"

He put the gun to his head. Panicked, I kept talking, paying no attention to the words that spilled out of my mouth. "I know you, Gabriel. I know you better than anyone in the world. You're strong. You're fearless. You're determined. I know you can get through this. And I'm here to help you. You need to put the gun down. Please."

I closed the distance between us. He trembled. I reached out as his hand came down, cautiously, and took the gun away. As soon as I set it on the counter, he fell into my arms, sobbing uncontrollably.

"We'll get you some help, Gabe. We'll get you help, I promise."

Nothing was more painful than holding my brother as he crumbled in my arms. Four weeks later, he took his own life.

"STOP THE FIGHT!" I yelled. "Stop the fight!"

Kaine grabbed me roughly. His voice was low, his tone sharp. "Keep your voice down!"

I jerked away from him.

"If you don't stop this fight," I began, teeth clenched. "I'll tell everyone here what you're doing to us."

"You wouldn't dare."

"Try me."

Kaine looked at the crowd surrounding us. Without a word, he pushed through the people to the cage, where Avan was awakening. I watched his dazed expression, and let out a breath when Kaine demanded that everyone leave.

The fight was done.

But Avan had lost.

What would happen now?

Chapter Fourteen

I washed our clothes in the bathtub. There was no shampoo or conditioner, only a small bar of soap with a seashell carved in the middle of it. It looked fancy, like those wrapped ones you found in a hotel bathroom. I took it from the ledge and filled the tub with warm water.

Avan lay sleeping in the next room, snoring softly. I washed his clothes first, his sweatpants and undershirt. A cloud of red seeped from the fabric as soon as I put them into the water.

"This may hurt just a little."

I lathered the clothing and scrubbed at the blood stains.

They punched him.

They threw him to the ground. They kicked him again and again. He coughed, gasped, struggled against the drugs.

I scrubbed harder, abandoning the bar of soap altogether and using my fingernails.

"I don't want to watch you get hurt anymore. I can't."

The water clouded with pink. I scrubbed and scrubbed until my wrists ached.

"You won't have to."

All at once, I saw what we'd experienced in the last two weeks with perfect clarity: Avan being beaten in front of me, Avan slipping on his own blood, Kaine raising the stick, Avan curling up, Avan hitting his head.

I grabbed my head with wet hands and screamed. My heart thudded in my ears. The bed creaked in the next room. I ran a hand over my hair and pressed my fist to my mouth, biting my knuckles willing myself to stay composed. Avan was waking up, and I needed to be there when he did.

I pulled myself together, hung his damp clothes on the shower rod, and walked towards the bed, sitting on the edge of the mattress. Avan faced away from me, snoring again. I put my hand on his shoulder.

"Avan, open your eyes."

No answer. I watched the blanket rise and fall with his shoulders. It was time to check his eyes. I'd learned from experience, from my brother's experience, that changes in pupils were a sign of brain damage.

"Avan, you have to wake up so I can check your eyes."

No response. My head ached and my muscles were sore. My patience was growing thin. I pulled at the blanket and raised my voice at him. "Get up!"

He grunted, audibly frustrated, tugging the blanket from my hand and up around his shoulder. I pressed my hands firmly over my eyes, my throat tight, my face hot. I needed to sleep. I needed to eat, to sleep in our bed, to breathe. I needed my paintbrush, my art studio, my empty canvases. I needed to paint everything that had happened, to document this torture chamber in splashes of color. I needed to ease my mind, but I couldn't do that now. Tears squeezed their way through my fingers. I couldn't do this.

It's just the concussion.

I took a deep breath, waited a few minutes, then gently shook Avan's shoulder.

"Avan, you need to get up. Please."

He heard me and rolled over slowly. The whites of his eyes were bloodshot. My fingers held his chin steady as I examined his pupils. I saw no change in their size. No brain damage.

"Thank God," I whispered.

His eyes were beginning to close already, his body seeking the rest he needed.

I didn't have it as easy. My stomach clenched. It lurched and rolled. I was going to throw up. I slid off the side of the bed, dizzy. My head whirled and I tripped over my own feet. I wasn't quick enough. I gagged and dry heaved on my hands and knees. My mouth burned and my eyes watered. Bile was all that came up.

I felt a hand touch my back. Avan was leaning over the side of the bed, soothing me, comforting me. I wiped my mouth with the back of my hand.

"Sorry,"

My arms shook. Avan moved my hair behind my ears. He forced a small chuckle. "It's okay, babe. Really, it's okay."

His voice was quiet and gentle, like he was. He rubbed my back. I crawled onto the bed, and together we lay back down, my head on his chest, his fingers through my hair. I closed my eyes.

Avan wasn't one to complain about his aches and pains, at least not in words. I'd hear a moan here, a groan there, after fight day, but never many, never loudly.

I opened my eyes when I felt him move. His free hand was to his head, his eyes closed, his brow furrowed. His mouth hardened.

"My head is killing me."

I shuddered against him. Back when he fought professionally, Avan would be given a forty-five day suspension after he suffered a concussion.

But now?

He had four days. He wasn't even trying to hide his pain from me anymore. His health was deteriorating. His composure was deteriorating with it.

Chapter Fifteen

A blast of frigid air hit me as Kaine opened my door.

"If you try anything," Kaine growled but didn't finish. He removed my hood and looked around him. He opened his jacket to reveal a pistol in the inside pocket, then made a pretend gun with the thumb and index finger of one hand. He pointed it in Avan's direction. He stayed silent for a long moment.

"BANG!"

I jumped at his voice, at his audacity, at his threat.

He laughed. He hid his pretend gun away, into his coat beside the real one, and led us into the warehouse.

No one was here. There were no cars except for the truck and there was no crowd. Avan's next opponent, who came in minutes after we did, was the only other human in sight.

Kaine placed a hand to Avan's chest, stopping him on his way into the cage. He then turned and spoke to the imaginary crowd.

"Fights end by knockout! No exceptions!"

Knockout?

No exception?

No witnesses.

Kaine had made it clear. If I tried to stop another fight, Avan would be killed. Avan made his way, unflinching, up the small staircase. I rushed after him, grabbing his arm. I felt a giant hand on my own arm.

"Let him go!" Kaine snapped.

I looked at him, my eyes pleading. "I need to talk to him for a minute."

Kaine shook his head.

"A second," I blurted. "It'll only take a second."

He began pulling me back. I snapped at him.

"Just give us a goddamn second!"

Kaine backed off. I pulled Avan aside.

"Listen to me," I whispered harshly. "Protect your head. Stay on your feet for as long as you can. He's got to get tired sometime. You can do this." I touched his chin. His facial hair was longer than he ever let it get before, a thick beard instead of his usual goatee. I brushed my fingers through it, letting them run across his cheek and stay there. "I know you can do this."

He blinked slowly. He leaned into my hand.

"That's enough!" Kaine said.

He grabbed my arm again and dragged me away. As the first round started, I knew I'd made a mistake.

Avan wasn't fighting back. He stood with his arms up, shielding his face. His opponent was relentless, throwing punches to Avan's injured body. Avan gritted his teeth and backed against the cage. When he finally returned punches, he swayed on his feet as if he were ready to collapse. His strikes were so weak they hardly affected the boy, and Avan knew it. He kept himself in motion to avoid receiving and throwing any more strikes; a perfect strategy - for a healthy fighter. I saw Avan would lose, that he would tire before the boy.

God, what had I done?

Avan could only hold his own for so long. I hadn't built him up when I took him aside. I'd torn him down. He couldn't win this. I knew he couldn't. All I'd done was set him up for failure.

A kick to the ribs, to the liver, sent Avan to his knees. He fell, his kneecap twisting slightly the wrong way as he landed. He stumbled to his feet but fell clumsily onto the canvas, holding his knee with both hands.

Something was wrong.

I froze, half expecting the boy to set upon Avan and punch him until he passed out. But he didn't. He stared at Avan, expression caught between regret and sympathy. The boy crouched, tapping his fingers on the canvas.

Avan and I both knew this gesture.

He was ending the fight.

"What the Hell do you think you're doing?" Kaine called out, angrily.

The boy looked up, his face stern.

"I'm tapping out!" he called back, standing.

Kaine unlocked the cage door and walked into the octagon, enraged. He towered over the boy.

"Fights end by knockout," he snapped. "No exceptions!"

The boy, no, not a boy. The young man, maybe eighteen, and making the first significant decision of his life, shook his head.

"I've hurt him badly enough."

He walked off, pushing past Kaine and making his way out. I ran to him. I threw my arms around his neck.

"Thank you," I sobbed, before I released him and hurried to Avan.

He lay in the center of the octagon, watching, his eyes shining. Out of the corner of my eye, I saw the men rush after the boy as he walked out of the warehouse.

Avan's knee had already started to swell. I helped him up. He clenched his teeth, hobbling even after I'd put his arm over my shoulder. A loud crack stopped us in our tracks, making us both jump. It was the unmistakable sound of a gunshot.

My knees gave out.

Avan and I dropped to the floor. Or at least, I thought that Avan was still beside me. I could feel his arms around me, my face against his shoulder. He was there with me, then he wasn't. My throat tightened. I couldn't feel him anymore. I could feel my bones inside my skin, feel the chill in the air, as reality faded in and out.

Avan brought me back, Avan whose voice was so full of rage I jerked in surprise.

"He was just a kid!"

The men had returned, minus the boy. Kaine looked at us through the chain links of the octagon and growled, "So was my son."

The words meant nothing to me, but they meant something to Avan.

I felt him tense beside me. His breathing became harsher, more rapid. I looked at him, taking note of the wetness in his eyes, but he didn't say anything.

Not when Kaine led us out of the warehouse with our hoods off.

Not when we saw the boy, prone on the cold asphalt in a pool of blood spreading beneath his gunshot-ruined skull.

It was only when we got back to the house, back into the basement, that Avan released his control. He hobbled to the nearest wall and sat against it. He curled up, buried his face into his hands, and screamed.

Chapter Sixteen

Avan wasn't talking, and I was scared. His headache had gotten significantly worse as time went on. I peered hopelessly into the empty bottle of painkillers. I turned off all the lights and sat beside him on the bed in the darkness.

The basement door opened and Kaine descended, a demon supervising our personal Hell. I leaned over and turned on one of the bedside lamps. Avan shielded his eyes with his arm and winced. I looked at Kaine. Trying not to snap, I said, "He needs more."

Kaine raised an eyebrow and laughed lightly. "More what?"

I rose up and held the empty bottle of painkillers at eye level. "Do I need to spell it out for you?"

No answer.

"He won't last much longer without them, not if you want him to fight!"

"We're all out." The calm, uncaring tone of Kaine's voice only made me angrier.

"What do you mean, 'You're all out?' We don't live in the jungle. Go to the drugstore and get more!"

"I mean we're all out!"

We both knew he was lying. He had the money to buy more. Why else would he be forcing Avan to continue to fight if not for the money? "Don't pull that!" I snapped. "I know you're lying!"

He smiled wider, and I couldn't feel the cold air in the basement anymore. My body was on fire. I don't know if it was anger or desperation that made me do what I did next. Perhaps it was both. I went up to Kaine, our captor, our tormentor, our judge and jury and executioner, and slapped him. I spat my words in his face.

"Just buy him more painkillers!"

He shoved me away from him and waved his finger in my direction. "You've crossed the line, bitch."

"I don't care," I growled through gritted teeth.

I felt Avan's fear, his anxiety growing with Kaine's anger and my rage. I heard the bed creak under his weight and fall onto the carpet. As I rushed to help him, concern overriding my anger, Kaine stomped up the stairs, slamming the door on his way out.

"God, Avan. Why? Why did you do that?" I demanded.

"He was gonna hurt you," he said, voice strained as I helped him onto the bed.

I sighed. I loved and hated Avan's desire to protect me, his willingness to put himself in harm's way for the sake of my well-being.

"I don't need protection, Avan. I need you to get better."

When he was settled into bed again, I looked at him, really looked at him. His wounds weren't healing. The cuts to his face, the bruises on his body, the tightness in his voice, none of them were healing as they should've been. Worst was his knee, swelled and angry and unable to support his weight for more than a few seconds.

He was slowly starving to death. We both were. Getting better wasn't an option for him anymore. I knew what I needed to do.

I bent down and untied my boot, sliding off my sock.

"Take a deep breath," I said, wrapping the sock around his knee. He did. He pressed his lips together, eyes squeezing shut as I tightened the sock around what I suspected was a torn ligament. It wouldn't help his pain, but it would at least keep the knee stable enough to walk on with my help. Or at least, that's what I hoped. Avan lifted his arm, hiding his eyes, his skin damp with chilled sweat. His jaw tightened.

"Sorry, babe, but I'm done," I soothed, sitting on the edge of the bed. "You're okay."

He let out a long, trembling sigh. My hand found his shin, my thumb rubbing against the dry skin.

"We need to get out of here, Avan. Now."

The basement door slammed open. Avan shot upward, his eyes alert, but slower than before. He eased off the bed and onto his feet, favoring his good leg, as the men reached the bottom of the stairs. He limped in front of me, protective, defiant. I grabbed his wrist, urging him to stay calm. Without looking at me, he spoke, his voice quiet, his tone rough.

"I'm not gonna let them hurt you."

I'd heard him say this before, and still believed him, still believed *in* him.

Kaine didn't hesitate. He walked straight up to Avan but stared at me. I froze, my fingers gripping Avan's wrist.

"Move," Kaine ordered.

Avan inhaled slowly. Though I was behind him, I thought I could feel his eyes burrow into Kaine, defying him without words. That was the thing about Avan. It was his eyes you had to watch out for, the change in his expression, that said all he needed to say.

As their silent battle waged on, I caught movement behind Kaine. The other men ferried stuff down the steps and set it all in the center of the room. Avan spoke slowly, harshly.

"If you lay one finger on her-"

"You'll do what?" Kaine interrupted. "Kill me?"

Avan's skin heated under my fingers. His pulse rose, and I could hear the rapid pounding of his heart. Maybe I was imagining it, but I didn't have time to figure it out.

Kaine made the first move, striking Avan in the face and knocking him down, his wrist slipping out of my hand. Kaine grabbed my hair, and I was dragged off the bed towards the middle of the room. There was a coil of rope, neatly rolled. Beside it sat the cane that Kaine whipped Avan with before. Finally, confusingly, was a massive tire, snow packed between the tracks. I fought and struggled, kicking and scratching, as Kaine pulled and dragged me along the floor.

"Don't touch her!" Avan yelled.

Out of the corner of my eye, I watched Avan lurch to his hands and knees. He surged forward but his knee gave way. He fell back on the floor with a grunt. Kaine stopped, still holding my hair. He turned his body slightly.

"What did you say?"

"Whip me!"

"I'm sorry?"

"I said," Avan replied, quieter now. "Whip me."

Kaine chuckled, letting me go. I fell to the ground, wincing.

"Avan, no!" I cried. I stumbled towards him. He rose on his good knee, catching me in his arms.

"Listen to me," he said, voice steady and calm. "I'll be fine, okay? It'll be over before you know it, I promise. I can take it."

"Avan-"

I didn't get to finish. He pressed his lips hard against mine before we were dragged apart.

"On your back."

Avan didn't hesitate. He eased to the floor and rolled onto his back. Kaine and a flunky picked up the tire and forced it over Avan's knees. I fell, overcome by dizziness, when I stood to stop them. It took three of them to lift Avan and flip him over before two tied Avan's wrists behind his back with the rope.

"Tie 'em tight," Kaine said, sounding giddy. "We don't want him squirming too much."

Avan lay with his cheek against the wood floor. He stared at me. "It's okay," he mouthed.

A calming sensation washed over me as I watched them tighten Avan's bonds, Kaine fastening his belt around Avan's ankles, and I struggled to name it. I finally sorted it out, recognizing it as what I'd felt when Avan surged forward to take my place: relief. I was *relieved* that it wasn't me. Close on its heels was shame.

Kaine's voice was low and deep, and my blood ran cold at his words.

"Tie her down."

Avan growled, more animal than human.

"If you hurt her, I swear to God-"

There was a loud *crack*! as Kaine struck the wall beside him with the cane. Before my ears stopped ringing, he'd gone to the bathroom and ran the sink. When he came out, the end of the cane was shiny with water, and I wondered why.

The men lifted and dragged me to a chair they'd placed in the corner. They forced me to sit down, to submit, and tied me down, their knots cutting my arms and legs. Kaine turned the tire so Avan and I were face to face, then tapped the arches of Avan's feet with the cane. Avan flinched and sucked in his breath at the same moment.

"Last chance to change your mind, Gutierrez."

Avan lifted his head. Our eyes locked for two powerful seconds before he bowed his head. His long hair fell over his ears, shielding his face from me.

"Just get it over with."

Something buckled inside me. Kaine looked my way.

"Let his agony be a lesson to you."

I'll never forget the force of the impact, the sharp *smack*! of the cane striking flesh, the agonized cry torn from Avan's mouth. Suddenly, I knew why Kaine wet the end. It increased the pain, the sting, the torment.

"Man up, Gutierrez!" the men taunted, as if Avan wasn't humiliated enough. "He didn't even hit you that hard!"

Avan's toes clenched and my feet burned in sympathy.

"Oh, he doesn't know what real pain is," Kaine said, preparing the next strike. "But I'll be glad to show him."

A sharper *smack!*, a louder cry, a labored gasp.

I fought against the ropes, fought and fought until the knots grew so tight I was sure they were cutting off my circulation. Avan hid his face from me, tucking his chin close to his chest. His hands were balled into quaking fists behind his back. His determination to hide his suffering was fighting his body's natural reaction and losing. He looked up, taking in my expression. In the short, bitter moment Kaine gave us between the pain, I watched Avan's lips curl up into a smile so faint I could hardly see it. It was forced, but it was there.

Though he meant to reassure, the gesture still stabbed. He had the strength to comfort me, even in his suffering. He willingly submitted to torture in my place, endured the agony, so I wouldn't have to. And I'd begged him not to do it out of fabricated selflessness. If I thought I could handle what came next, I was wrong in a thousand ways.

"Beat 'im raw!" one of the men urged.

That's exactly what he did. Mercilessly, relentlessly, Kaine showered Avan's feet with lashes. Everything inside me ripped open, wounds that bled when Avan screamed and didn't stop. He strained to keep still, to keep quiet. Every muscle was visible, every vein protruded, his natural instincts pleading for him to get away. One foot curled behind the other, unable to withstand the abuse. When the other foot curled with nowhere to hide, Avan kicked.

"You're gonna kill him!" I shouted. "Stop! Please!"

Smack! Smack! Smack!

Every lash sent a wave of crippling anguish through me. Kaine may as well have forced me into the tire and whipped me. I couldn't watch this anymore.

"AVAN!"

He is the calm within my storms.

Stop

His breathing brings me back to me.

Hurting

He takes me in his arms, safe and warm.

Me
"It's okay," he whispers. "It's okay."

TIME PLAYS TRICKS ON you. The beating lasted moments that were an eternity. That's how long it took for the cane to snap under the weight of Kaine's brutality. By the time the frail wood succumbed, Avan had been lashed at least twenty times, maybe more. I didn't have a count for all the slashes it left in my soul.

"Do you want me to stop?" Kaine turned his gaze to meet mine.

I could only nod, my body trembling with sobs. Avan made no sound. He'd passed out just moments ago, his cheek against the floor, his body limp.

"Then learn to behave."

The bits of broken bamboo were thrown aside, the men freed Avan's wrists and ankles, turned him over, and removed the tire from his knees. I prayed Avan would remain unconscious until the men untied me, but his body wasn't so merciful.

Avan moaned softly as he awoke. They gripped his arms and forced him to stand, adding torment to his humiliation. With a rasp, Avan lifted his head and I saw the suffering in his eyes. His knees buckled and he collapsed. The men laughed when he grabbed his lower leg.

Kaine heaved the tire into his arms and motioned to the stairs with a jerk of his head. He stepped over Avan, catching him with the toe of his boot as he did. The others followed, leaving me tied to the chair and Avan curled up, broken and beaten on the floor.

Chapter Seventeen

Avan untied me. Avan, who had endured a vicious lashing. Avan, who had cried out with every blow. Avan, who was so selfless that he was willing to do anything for me.

Anything.

He fell several times in his attempt to get to me. He fumbled at the knots with hands that shook so he could hardly keep his grip on the rope. With a grunt of frustration, he used his teeth. With my right hand free, I helped pull the other knots loose.

"Avan, I'm sorry!" I sobbed, taking him into my arms. "God, I'm so stupid. I'm sorry! I didn't know what else to do."

His fingers dug into my shoulders. He buried his face into my hair, his breath hot, his body convulsing in my arms. His mouth pressed harder into my shoulder, and I made my decision when his choked-back sounds of pain reached my ears.

I stood and stripped the bed, carrying the blanket, sheets, and pillows into the bathroom. I turned on the bathwater and waited for it to warm. When the tub filled, I made my way back, crouching over Avan and lightening my voice as if speaking to a child.

"Avan, sweetheart. I need you to walk with me. Can you do that?"

Without letting him answer, I pulled his arm over my shoulder and eased him to his feet.

The walk to the bathroom was slow and painful. Avan's legs threatened to buckle with each step, his gait hobbled, balance nonexistent.

"Just a few more steps," I reassured him, though I knew those few steps would be agony.

His knee gave out. He stumbled, nearly falling into the doorway. I clutched him tighter, unwilling to let him give up. When he was finally in the tub, in the warm soothing water, a look of relief bloomed on his face. I climbed in with him. I wrapped my arms around his shoulders. He lay his head against me, his eyes closed, his body relaxing. He inhaled, shaky, and reached down to grab his toes. His voice was breathy.

"I can't feel them anymore."

"Your toes?"

"My feet."

A sudden weight crushed against my chest. His feet hadn't only been whipped raw. They'd been whipped numb, and it frightened him. Avan, who faced men larger and stronger than himself in the octagon. Avan, who feared nothing. This? This scared him, and a searing hatred filled me. It wasn't mere hatred for our captors, the ones who had hurt him. No. It was hatred for myself, the one who had let it happen, the one who didn't stop it, the one who sat by and watched in relief.

I took the hand that gripped his toes and rested it over my breast. His fingers curled closed under my palm as if holding onto my heartbeat.

"Can you feel *that*?" I whispered.

After a moment, his hand opened, his damp fingers spreading across the bare skin of my collarbone, and I let my fingers press his hand closer to my chest. He didn't smile, but softly tapped his index finger to the beat of my heart. The gesture, so soothing, so effortless, felt more intimate than making love.

As in tune as we were during these moments of complete trust and vulnerability, moments like this strengthened our connection more. The feeling of his skin against my own, the soft touches, led to greater intimacy than sex. I rocked him, singing softly to him until the water grew cold.

Our skin pruned beneath our clothes. I helped Avan out of the tub and sat him on the toilet lid. Taking the blanket from the floor, I wrapped it tightly around Avan's shoulders, then pulled off my wet clothes, leaving me in my bra and panties. I crouched in front of Avan, drawing his hands to my chest, willing him to focus only on my heartbeat.

When I was sure he was dry enough, that he wasn't in danger of going into shock, I guided him back to the now-dry tub and lay down. It was cramped and cold, but Avan couldn't walk to the bedroom, and I certainly couldn't leave him alone.

He mumbled my name.

"What is it?" I asked him.

He slowly sucked in his breath. In a calm voice, he said something that shook everything I thought I knew. "You need to leave me here. When he comes back, get out and run as fast as you can. Don't wait for me. Just run."

In the end, I stayed.

Chapter Eighteen

I probably should've listened, should've run away like the coward that I was, but I stayed. If I had run, I wouldn't have been forced to face the next round of lashes. I would've been spared the devastation of watching Avan deteriorate. I wouldn't have said the things I said, done the things I'd done, things that would save Avan's life and threaten mine. And maybe, just maybe, I wouldn't have had to cope with the horrifying secret that spilled from Avan's mouth.

"WHAT IS THIS CALLED again?" I asked, struggling under the weight of my headgear and gloves.

Avan smirked at my frown.

"Sparring," he answered.

He stood a distance from me, dressed in red shorts and a white muscle shirt, his feet bare. I wore my white shorts and red sports bra, my hair tied back. Around me, I heard the grunts of men and women, lifting and sparring, running and jumping in the gym.

"Okay, "I said, voice trembling.

I had no reason to be nervous. Avan was careful to explain every rule to me, making sure I knew when to tap out, even placing me into a chokehold, pressing and squeezing hard enough for me to tap the moment I felt faint. I was so vulnerable with his legs around my waist, his arm over my throat, my life in his hands. I had been completely under his control.

"Are ya scared?"

Something struck me in the stomach. A fist? A bat?

No.

I realized it was grief. The last time I heard these words was seventeen years ago, from my dead brother's mouth. I couldn't cry in front of Avan and ruin the day he'd anticipated all week. The excitement was written all over his face now. I couldn't take that away from him.

I swallowed my pain and attempted to mirror Avan's smirk.

"I'm not scared of anything."

"Oh, come on," Avan insisted. "You're scared of everything!"

He didn't cruelly say this. It was a challenge. I shot him the same look I'd given my brother all those years ago. He adjusted his stance, feet slightly apart, knees bent, fists up.

"Remember," he said, all playfulness aside. "If you feel any pain, just say our safe word and I'll-"

I charged. I tackled him, slamming him onto the mat. His face was shocked, his light eyes wide. I smiled down at him, raising my eyebrows.

"Oops, my foot slipped," I said, unsympathetically.

He smiled his crooked smile, trying to sound hurt and threatening, and failing miserably.

"Oh, you are so gonna get it."

I lowered myself over him, my lips just inches from his face. I kept my voice low, seductive, taunting.

"You'll have to pin me first."

He leaned in and kissed me, his lips brushing the skin beneath my ear. His hands, so gentle, slid down to my waist. When he spoke, his voice mirrored my own.

"Number one rule." He breathed in sharply and I was flipped onto my back before I could process what happened. He pinned my arms down onto the mat, flashing a cheeky grin. "Never lose focus."

I wrapped my legs around him and twisted my hips to no avail.

"Stop laughing!" I said.

Before I knew it, we were wrestling, our bodies tangled into each other in a mess of sweat and skin. As usual, Avan had the upper hand. I struggled to get out from under him, both laughing the entire time.

Suddenly, I was eight years old again, wrestling on the stained twin mattress with my brother. The memory came and went, Gabe's face flashing over Avan's. Only then did I notice the similarities between my brother and the man I now shared my life with, his playfulness, the way he teased and tricked me, his compulsive drive to be perfect, his unwavering determination and will. I'd lost it all after Gabe had taken his own life, and I'd gained it all back on the day I met Avan. In that moment, the piece of me that had died with Gabe was reborn. At that moment, I felt whole again.

When Avan's face came into view, it was him again. Just Avan. He sat up on his knees, still on top of me and I gazed up at him with admiring eyes. My hands found his legs. Slowly, I let my fingers slide up his thighs, my nails teasing the warm skin beneath his shorts. He inhaled, shuddering with hunger, with lust, with wanting. I seized my chance, sitting up swiftly and pinning his arms to the mat.

"Never lose focus," I said. "Number one rule, remember?"

This time, he didn't look shocked. He looked pleased, joyful, and proud.

"I've taught you well."

I was aware of the other people in the gym, grunting and wrestling, but they seemed very far away. When I leaned in and kissed the man I loved, the man I was certain I would spend the rest of my life with, it was easy to believe that the rest of the world had melted away.

I WOKE TO FIND AVAN'S fingers knotted in my own, our legs tangled, our noses nearly touching. We had buried our heads against one another in our half-sleep. As I lay there, watching Avan's breathing move the dark flyaway hairs by his face, I imagined a baby between us, a gorgeous little life, the perfect combination of Avan and me. I saw it so clearly: a beautiful baby boy with my pale eyes and Avan's curly black hair, with my delicate nose and Avan's slender fingers, with my laugh and Avan's smile. He would be perfect, and I knew exactly what we would name him.

The tub, which had felt so cold before, was stuffy and hot. Even the blanket beneath us felt warm. I don't know how long I luxuriated in the heat before noticing how tightly Avan's eyes were closed, how badly his body shook, no, quaked.

"Avan," I said, alarmed. "What's wrong?"

His voice broke, his breathing choppy and fast.

"Co-ld."

It was all he said, "Cold," but his body was boiling. He was spiking a fever!

I practically leaped out of the bathtub, and tucked the blanket around him as best I could. His jaw tightened, his shivering worsening as he broke into a sweat. Now that I wasn't beside him, I could feel how cold and unforgiving the basement had become. Kaine had left the air conditioner on again.

Damn you, Kaine. Damn you!

Avan needed to be warmer. I needed to do something now to break his fever, but what? The only blanket we had was wrapped around Avan, and we had no access to any other heat source.

Normally, I couldn't wait for winter. I had looked forward to watching the snow fall in beautiful, delicate flakes from my bedroom window since childhood, a blanket snugged around me, a hot drink in my hands. I loved the cold. Now, for the first time in my life, I wanted to taste the heat of summer more than anything.

I sat at the edge of the tub, feeling sorry for myself, watching Avan shiver. Unlike me, he preferred warmth, often standing in the shower until the water became so hot the bathroom grew muggy and unbearable.

The shower!

I jumped from the tub, closed the door, and helped Avan out, sitting him on the floor. As soon as I turned the knob, felt the heat of the water spraying from the grimy showerhead, I knew it was the solution. I sat behind Avan, hugging his shoulders, praying that steam would accumulate soon. As small as the bathroom was, the comforting warmth quickly rose into a suffocating heat that made the air sticky and heavy. Within minutes, Avan let out a breath.

"You're a genius," he said with a light laugh.

I pressed my cheek against his back, lending him as much of my body heat as I could. When he finally stopped shivering, I sighed with relief. The beat of his heart, so faint, carried through his back to my cheek. Greedily, I took it in, his heartbeat, his breathing, the evidence he was still alive.

Avan and I jerked when the bathroom door opened. The men stood in the doorway, hoods and zip-ties in hand. My words slipped out before I had the chance to stop them.

"Don't you dare touch him!"

I tightened my grip around Avan. Kaine laughed and stepped further into the bathroom. He crouched before us.

"He's got a fight tonight."

Tonight?

Avan's last fight was only a day ago. Kaine said Avan would get four days of recovery. No! It couldn't be tonight. This wasn't part of the deal!

"He can't walk!" I snapped. "What makes you think he can fight?"

Looking at Avan instead of me, Kaine reached into his pocket, pulling out his knife. He placed the end of the blade against my elbow. I didn't flinch.

"I'll do it," Avan said, panicked. "I'll fight!"

He straightened himself and began to rise, bracing one hand on the edge of the tub to steady himself. My words came ahead of my thoughts again.

"Avan, no! You can't!"

Despite my protest, he limped forward, gripping the corner of the counter to keep himself from falling, to convince me he could do this. The men grabbed him, threw the hood over his head, and forced him out of the bathroom. Avan stumbled and fell. They jerked him up and began climbing the stairs. Kaine looked at me with his dead black eyes. He smirked, and something snapped inside me.

Chapter Nineteen

I lunged at Kaine, clawing at his face. My muscles, or what was left of them, burned and tired from the effort. When he smacked my hands away, I was too weak to fight him off. He overpowered me, bashing my head into the sink. I recovered seconds later to see him crouching over me, his hands around my throat.

"You shouldn't have done that," he said, shaking his head. "You really shouldn't have done that!"

I squirmed. He straddled me with his legs, trapping me under him. My feet slipped against the slick floor.

"You know what I could do to that little boy toy of yours? I could take this knife and cut his pretty little face. Or I could whip him until his feet are nothing but bloody slabs of meat."

No, not Avan. Anything but Avan!

"I'll listen," I gasped, trying to pry his hand away. "I promise!"

He looked away, just for a moment. My lungs burned and cried for air.

"It's too late." Kaine climbed off me, leaving me gasping, choking, fighting for air. "I'll think of something."

With a huff, Kaine walked out of the bathroom. I was left on the floor, writhing, holding my throat, wondering what he would do next. I heard the basement door slam. What happened next was excruciating; thud after muffled thud, the sound of Avan being punched, kicked, and thrown against the floor. They were beating him because of me, because of my actions.

I bolted up the stairs. "Stop it," I begged, pounding on the door. "Stop hurting him, please!"

The thuds only continued, growing louder and louder, each one followed by a cry of pain. I didn't need to wonder what Kaine had planned for me now. This was my punishment. Avan wasn't strong enough to fight them off himself. Not anymore.

Why him?

Why him and not me?

It hit me like a frigid gust of wind: Kaine refusing to give Avan the painkillers, Kaine being completely unfazed when Avan was hurt, Kaine whipping Avan until his walking was hindered. He was making bets against him, earning money at Avan's expense. That had to be it. It had to be!

It didn't do me any good, not at the moment, not listening as the beating continued.

Then stopped.

Silence. It was louder than the thuds, louder than Avan's distress, louder than everything. I waited. And waited.

At last the door opened, and as they did on our first day in this basement, the men shoved Avan to the floor. He lay there, still, quiet, dark, defeated.

"Oh my God," I gasped, climbing off the bed. "Avan."

I slid onto my knees, my hands hovering over him, wanting to touch him, not wanting to touch him. I held my breath and removed the hood. Blood was everywhere in his hair, on his face, his shoulders, his chest. It was even in his ears. I tucked his hair behind his ear. There was a gash on his cheek.

"Lost a lot of blood tonight," Kaine said, smiling. "Might want to clean him up."

He laughed. I didn't watch him walk up the stairs. I didn't hear the door close. My focus was on Avan.

God, what had they done to him?

"Avan," I whispered. "Look at me. Please."

He did. He rose slowly onto his knees, weak and trembling. His face was so swollen, so bloodied I hardly recognized him.

"Did they break anything?" I asked, fighting to present the pretense of strength for us both.

He didn't answer. He straightened himself, wincing, and closed his arms around me. A sound of distress, muffled and strained, found my ears when I hugged him back. It came from Avan, who buried his face in my shoulder to smother it. Anxiety shot through me, but as I pulled away, Avan locked his arms tighter around me.

"Not yet," he begged, squeezing me to him. His hold was so tight that I had difficulty breathing, and I heard that awful, piteous sound again. "Don't let go," he continued softly. "Please, don't let go."

And I didn't.

"I've got you, Avan," I said, holding him tighter. "You're okay. I've got you."

For the briefest moment, we were Jack and Rose, struggling to stay afloat on a sinking ship. I was on the floating door, hopeless and terrified but alive. Avan was in the water, fighting to hold on, in danger of sinking deep into the depths of that dark and frozen sea.

The dark fantasy dissolved as I found the break. He sat on the edge of the tub and grabbed at his side. The same distressing sound hit my ears again, no longer muffled. I looked down. A long, dark bruise was painted along the bottom half of his ribcage. I must've bumped it while easing him down.

I knelt, pressing my fingers gently to the swollen, tender mess of purple. Avan flinched. He sucked in sharply and panic rose within me. They had broken his ribs, at least one. I felt it, the bones shifting under my fingers, the fractures hidden under his thinning muscles.

"Can you breathe?" I asked, tears welling in my eyes.

He nodded, exhaling slowly, his eyes shut tight, fingers gripping the side of the tub. I rested my hands on his good knee and pressed my quivering lips against his fingers.

God, how much longer would I have to see him like this?

Keep it together.

Keep it together!

Avan opened his eyes. His expression softened at the sight of me breaking in front of him. In a silky voice, he comforted me.

"It's not your fault."

But it *was* my fault.

What else would they do to him if I disobeyed?

Would they break his fingers? Shatter his eye socket? Crush his hand? Would they beat him to death?

I wanted to tell him my fears, to shed my anxiety as one sheds a winter coat, but all I could manage was, "Let's get you cleaned up."

He forced a smile and I returned it as falsely.

I thought this was my punishment, Kaine's way of getting back at me, but something inside me said, "He's not done yet."

When the men came back hours later, carrying rope, a tarp, and two weapons I couldn't identify, I knew my fears had come true.

Chapter Twenty

Avan's wrists were bound to the wooden post of the bed, a clear tarp thrown onto the floor behind him. I couldn't keep my eyes off it. It was Kaine who put it there, Kaine who stood near Avan now, holding a long thick stick in his hand - a whipping staff.

"For the mess," Kaine said, smiling pleasantly, as though he'd spilled wine on a table and added a few bucks to the tip.

Outraged, I struggled against the men, who held me so tightly that my skin had gone red.

"Get away from him!" I snarled.

As if obeying my command, Kaine stepped back. Then, he held the staff out to me.

"Strike him."

My brain connected the dots. Avan's tightly bound wrists, the whipping staff, the careful consideration Kaine had taken to ensure that nothing would stain the dusky orange carpet.

Strike him... Strike him!

This was my punishment.

A chill passed through me, dulling some senses and heightening others. Every sound was muffled by the ringing in my ears. The men's grip loosened, and I felt the weight of the staff in my hands, the thudding of my heart.

"No!" I dropped the staff from nerveless fingers. "I won't do it. You can't make me!"

Then I glimpsed a gun's barrel. Kaine's voice, cold, oily, and dark, whispered in my ear.

"Strike him." One of the men picked up the staff and placed it in my hands. "Or *I* will."

Or I will.

I replayed the words over and over in my head until I finally understood. My mind played back the last time Kaine had whipped Avan. I relived the viciousness, the agony, and fighting to keep Avan alive.

This staff wasn't a whipping cane. It wasn't an instrument that left welts on the body. It was a whip that left deep cuts in its wake, a whip that could kill if used with enough brutality and force. Kaine wasn't the type to show mercy. He'd whip Avan to death if I didn't comply.

Still, I hesitated.

Avan knelt with his head bowed, the muscles of his back tight, bracing for the first lash. His shoulders trembled. When I spoke, my emotions betrayed me, my voice little more than a choked sob.

"Av?"

Avan swallowed hard. "It's okay, angel."

I trembled. My breathing quickened, my chest tight, my knees weak. Avan nicknamed me Angel on the day we'd met. He'd used it ever since, but only in private, never in public. How could I possibly hurt him?

Kaine heaved a sigh of impatience. I felt the cold steel of the muzzle of the gun against my back. I took a deep breath and closed my eyes.

"Now," he growled.

I opened my weeping eyes and delivered the first lash.

The staff made a solid *thud* as it hit Avan's body. His head jerked up, back arching in a rapid, unnatural movement. A deep grunt escaped from the back of his throat. I cringed and whimpered, nearly dropping the staff again.

"No, no, no," Kaine said. "That doesn't count."

I saw the reddish-brown welt rising across Avan's back and turned away. Kaine pointed the gun in my face.

"You've got to put your back into it," he whispered harshly. "Like you mean it."

I swallowed.

If I die, there's no hope for Avan, I rationalized.

"Back off," I hissed at Kaine, jabbing at him with the staff. He jumped back, surprised. "You want me to do this? Fine. I'll do it, but I'll do it my way."

He grunted, but he gave me the space I wanted. I'd done it; I'd made a demand and he'd given in.

I adjusted my stance, ensuring I wouldn't hit the same spot, then struck Avan, my gentle Avan, with more force. He choked back a cry. His fingernails dug into the wood of the bedpost.

I thought I was going to throw up.

Kaine grunted in frustration. He stepped forward and pressed the gun to the back of Avan's head.

"Strike him!" he roared. "Lash him or I will!"

"Get out of the way, then!" I returned his fury with my own, fury at what he was forcing me to do, fury at the pain I would inflict. I couldn't hold back the tears anymore. They dripped and burned down my cheeks. But Kaine complied, stepping away, watching me.

The whipping staff shook in my hands as I tightened my grip.

Kaine grinned, a horrid, evil thing.

"Avan," I whispered, tears still flowing. "I'm sorry."

With a voice trembling and strained, Avan said, "It's okay, angel. Do what you've got to do."

I loved him. God, I loved him. And to save him, I had to hurt him.

A larger welt was rising on his lower back. Kaine, trying to keep control but unwilling to get within range of the staff again, kept the gun pointed in Avan's direction, finger on the trigger.

What else could I do?

I closed my eyes, raised my arms, and swung the staff.

This *thud* was wet. Avan cried out, a brief, agonized scream, and my legs threatened to buckle beneath me.

"Good girl!" Kaine praised, gun holstered, clapping wildly. "That's the way to do it!"

The other men hooted and clapped along, as if I'd knocked out my opponent in the ring. I opened my eyes, then looked away, pressing a hand over my mouth. The wound was devastating, a deep bleeding gash beneath Avan's shoulder blades.

Somehow, as the men continued their praises, I found the courage to look back towards Avan. Through the mess of red, I could see just how deep my blow had cut into his skin. The soft tissues, the thin layer of muscle, were sliced clean through, exposed to the frigid air of this basement.

God, I had done that!

"One down," Kaine said, enthusiastically. He clapped. And the more he clapped, the harder he praised, the greater the anger rose inside me.

Avan coughed, struggling to keep his grip on the bedpost. Soft, choked noises, like he was resisting the urge to weep, resisting the urge to vomit, fell from his mouth.

My senses, already hyperalert, focused on Avan's body. I smelled his blood first, heavy and metallic. Then, his sweat, musky and sharp. My vision sharpened without warning, my eyes searching his back, his badly bruised skin, the thick red trail running down his back and dripping onto the tarp.

When Avan said my name, barely more than a whisper, I snapped.

I turned and screamed, swinging the staff this way and that, forcing the men back a step, then another, and another. Kaine raised his hands as if in surrender, a small smile on his face. There was a spot of blood under his eye. In passing, I wondered how it got there. When I glanced down at the staff, red with Avan's blood, I knew.

"Get the fuck back!" I shouted, my teeth bared.

Avan was saying my name, but I wasn't listening. I needed to protect him, to *save* him.

"Didn't think you had it in ya," Kaine said, chuckling. He didn't look afraid. He looked amused, as if my fit of rage was nothing but a joke to him, a kitten fighting a snake. He had the gun in his hand again, but he held it casually, unworried.

Why? I wondered. I still had the staff. I could've struck him, knocked the gun from his hand.

Then what? Was I willing to take the life of another human being? Could I live with that knowledge, with that guilt? Even when that same human belittled and tortured me and the person I loved?

Would it eat me alive?

When I looked deep within, I knew the answer. I lowered the staff and said, "No more."

Kaine wiped the blood from his cheek with his sleeve, then cacked each of the knuckles on his right hand slowly, deliberately, before speaking.

"Fine. You win. No more."

Hope welled in my breast, and for a moment a surge of elation filled me. Then Kaine continued speaking.

"For him. But you? You will take the rest of his lashes. He will not be touched."

I opened my mouth to protest but the words caught on my tongue when I heard Avan draw in a breath. I half expected him to speak out in my defense, to willfully take my place as he'd done time and time again. Instead, his broken voice choked the words I never expected to hear.

"I–I can't do this any more. I'm s-sorry, angel. I ca–can't."

Those raspy words, that winded voice, sent a frigid twinge through my already frozen body. Piece by piece, my heart shattered. Shame, anger, and guilt burned inside of me.

Was I really going to whip Avan to death out of cowardice? No...

Despite the sick feeling that tore through my stomach, I slowly nodded.

They tied me to the support beam in his place, hung directly above the tarp on the floor. My shirt was torn from my body, my arms high above my head. The black hood made it impossible to see where the first lash would come from. I breathed slowly, remembering what Avan had taught me. I shivered from the cold, from the fear.

A whimper escaped me.

No! I won't give these bastards the satisfaction! I fell silent, clenching my teeth.

When the first lash was delivered across my breast and collar bone, my lungs tore open in an explosive burst, but not a sound, not a cry, did I make. Avan's voice was ringing in the background, desperate, begging them to stop.

Better me than him.

The pain was blinding, instantaneous, excruciating.

Better me than him.

Welts rose under my skin. They broke open.

Better me than him.

My vision blurred. My head slumped forward.

Better me than...

Chapter Twenty-One

I awoke to the blade of a knife. It was orange. Why was it orange? I blinked and saw the flame, a warm flash of brightness in the cold gray air.

How had I survived?

Kaine knelt and pressed the searing metal to Avan's wound. The sizzle of Avan's tormented flesh, the stench of his scorched skin, dove into my senses and would haunt my nightmares for years to come. I blacked out before I heard him scream.

When I came to, my eyes took in the face in front of me, the blade glowing in Kain's hand, the realization it was my turn. I gritted my teeth. My skin burned. I cried out, then it all went dark again.

Seconds, or minutes or hours or days later, I awoke. Everything was out of focus, the images flickering and dimming before reappearing.

Kaine picked up the whipping staff. Avan was a dark, blurry figure, slumped forward, and unconscious.

Or dead.

The men untied him and lifted his legs. The soles of his feet were exposed to Kaine, to the whip. My vision cleared in time to see Avan's eyes, his beautiful green eyes, flutter open. They widened as the lashes were administered one after another, a spray of crimson spurting after each one.

No... No! Kain had promised me that Avan would be spared.

"St-stop!" I yelled, weakly.

Avan struggled. Watching him uselessly twist and jerk was like watching an innocent dog being beaten to death during the Yulin festival in China. His hands strained to block the whip. He screamed. And I blacked out again.

I awoke on the floor.

My nose immediately registered the scent of blood and burned flesh. In the distance, I heard the door slam. My vision cleared again, taking in the image of Avan laying unresponsive in front of me. Even from this angle, I could see the long pink burn mark on his back and the blood on his feet.

One arm was stretched in front of him, as if he'd attempted to reach me before passing out. I reached for him, my chest on fire, and touched his hand with my fingertips. He groaned softly.

His head lifted heavily, as if it took every ounce of strength to do so. I squeezed his fingers gently. His eyes watered, tears sliding silently down his cheek, as he released my hand. He pulled away, burying his face into his arm, then did something I'd never heard him do before.

He sobbed.

This man, this solid, unstoppable force who'd defeated countless numbers of men in the cage, crumbled before my eyes.

Chapter Twenty Two

The bath became our savior.

Through the pain, I washed our wounds. Through the pain, I wrapped Avan's feet with the shredded pieces of my shirt. Through the pain, I watched his eyes fill with tears, then blink them away at the last moment.

He wanted to speak, I could see it. But he stayed quiet, his fingers in my hair, mine in his. Our foreheads rested together as we lay in the bathtub, waiting for our wounds to heal, waiting for rescue, and, somewhere in the back of our minds, we waited for death.

My chest, my ribs, my belly burned. A searing heat spread through me with every breath, preventing me from getting the sleep I craved. I knew Avan's countless wounds were keeping him from sleeping too.

His ribs were visible now, the bones of his hips and shoulders protruding. It was as if his skin were nothing more than a thin sheet hung over his skeletal frame. I imagined myself looking like him, my eyes sunken, my lips cracked, my eyes empty of hope.

"Go," he mouthed.

I shook my head against the blanket beneath us. Leaving him behind was out of the question.

"We go together, or not at all," I hissed.

He whispered my name, his hand running over my hair. His words came in a sharp, almost angry whisper.

"I *can't* walk."

With a jolt I realized he was right. It had taken everything in me to get him to the bathroom. How would I get him upstairs, drag him through the woods, through the snow, and carry him down the busy highway until I flagged down a car?

It was all speculation anyway. I didn't know what was out there, just what I constructed from my imaginings. Was it enough to bet our lives on? Because I smelled pine trees? Because I *thought* I heard the distant whooshing of cars?

Then again, if we stayed here, we would die.

That was certain.

Attempting an escape wasn't a question, no matter what I faced outside. No, the bigger question was would Avan be strong enough to survive the journey?

I shook my head again, harder this time, shooing away my questions and doubts like they were gnats, and focused on Avan instead.

"I'm not leaving you," I whispered back, fisting a handful of his hair.

It was greasy now, his curls matted from lack of washing. Perhaps mine was like that, too. My hair was tangled, I knew, but Avan's fingers were so gentle that it was easy to forget. His long beautiful fingers, his hands, his soul, his being, were so precious to me. As I pulled my hand away, a clump of his hair came with it, black wispy strands caught between my fingers. They'd come out so easily. He didn't seem to notice, or care. He just looked at me, eyes intense.

"I. Can't. Walk." He emphasized every word.

As much as I loved him, I fought him. As much as I knew he was right, I fought him. I would keep fighting him.

Why?

Loyalty.

It was an attribute ingrained in me as a little girl. Loyalty to each other was everything to my family, and so it passed to me. I wasn't ready to throw that away. Yet if I didn't attempt to leave, to find help? My best friend, my lover, my future husband and father of my children, would die.

The loss of my brother had damaged me to the point where I doubted I would ever be whole again. That was before I met Avan. Before I discovered pieces of my brother in him. Losing him would be like losing Gabriel all over again. Losing Avan would leave me forever broken beyond repair.

I blinked the tears from my eyes. I inhaled slowly, took his face in my hands, and kissed him. I didn't tell him that I loved him. I didn't fill him with false hope by reassuring him everything would be okay.

I looked into his eyes, my voice strong and steady as I said, "Stay alive for me."

Chapter Twenty-Three

The basement door was left open. The padlock was gone. It was like Kaine wanted us to escape, or wanted me to escape, or...

The thought came to me suddenly, remembering Kaine's sadistic nature. Or, to leave Avan behind with no protection. Could he be that devious? Of course he could, but I didn't contemplate it for long. There was no time.

My body screamed with every step, my skin painful and tight where my wounds had been cauterized. I had to move quickly, but I couldn't move quickly. I glanced back towards the bathroom, mouthed "I'm sorry," opened the door, and peered down the hall.

No one in sight.

This was the first time I'd seen the upstairs, and I was taken aback. The house was surprisingly homey and comfortable, all browns and reds and oranges, plaid furniture and shiny blonde wood as far as the eye could see. If we weren't held against our will, I probably would've loved it. Light spilled in through the wall of windows in the living room, and I thought I could see the faint outline of trees far in the distance.

There *were* woods. If I was right about them, then the snow-dusted dirt path that stretched from the driveway to the woods had to lead to a highway. It had to!

I was suddenly filled with hope. Immediately, my dreams seemed more reachable. The thought of marrying Avan and bearing his children felt more real now, but the snowflakes were still falling, heavy and relentless, threatening to engulf those dreams.

How long before the path would be completely buried again? How long before the snow became too deep to maneuver through?

I realized I'd fallen too deep into my thoughts with the slam of a door. A dented red truck had pulled into the driveway and men were walking towards the front door. I scrambled, rushed into the first room I found, and softly shut the door.

The room smelled dusty and unused but looked cozy. It was dim, a single lamp weakly illuminating the paperwork on the desk and the photographs stuck every which way on the wall above it. I stepped forward, squinting at the photos. It was a mess of tape and pushpins, paper clips and staples.

They weren't only photos. There were newspaper clippings, tattered and brown, the print too distorted to read. With a start, I recognized the boy in the black and white picture on the closest clipping

It was Avan!

I shifted my attention to the photo. A young Avan stood with his hands behind his head, his eyes alert, his expression panicked. My eyes followed his frightened gaze to a team of medics kneeling over the other boy, lying on the floor of the cage. A gush of sympathy for this boyish Avan rushed through me. He was a deer in headlights, paralyzed, frozen in place, unable to move away from the collision that would end his life.

The other boy, the boy he'd taken down, was surrounded by medical personnel, and I saw that they were working on him with a sense of urgency. I understood the need, for there was another picture of him, lying in a hospital bed with a tube down his throat, in the far right corner.

Had Avan done that?

No, he couldn't have done it. He wouldn't have done it!

"Death In the Cage!"

My eyes scanned the headline again, my brain thinking-hoping that I had read it wrong.

"I took that photo on the last day I saw him."

I turned to see Kaine standing behind me, his eyes on the photo.

"Do you know what it's like," he began, tears filling his eyes, "to watch the one you love the most die before your eyes?"

I did. But I wasn't about to admit that. He stepped closer, his eyes not leaving the photo. He pointed a fat finger towards the photos of Avan.

"He ruined my life when he went for that kick. He destroyed me when he murdered my son!"

I looked at Avan again, young, skinny, fragile Avan. I said quietly, "I don't believe you."

He looked at me, his eyes burning with hatred.

"Why don't you let that monster tell you for himself!" he snarled, gripping my arm.

Like a marionette, I let him take me down the stairs. I don't know why I didn't try to run, to fight, to escape. Perhaps I wanted, needed, to hear Avan's take on the whole thing, to hear his denial... or his confession.

Chapter Twenty-Four

"Tell her." Kaine said.

Avan looked at us, lifting his head from the blanket. He hadn't moved an inch since I'd left. He laid there, waiting. Waiting for me or waiting to die, I didn't know. He flinched at Kaine's sharp tone.

"Tell her what you did, Gutierrez!"

Avan stayed silent, his eyes darting from Kaine to me. It was then that I saw the dark circles, so dark they were almost black, surrounding his eyes.

How had I not noticed them before?

His dark olive complexion was replaced with pale and chalky skin. There were small streaks of gray in his hair. His cheeks were shadowed by his cheekbones. His beard was speckled with white. Even his hands looked frail as they shook uncontrollably. I could count every bone in his fingers, his skin leathery and waxy.

How had I not noticed?

Kaine grabbed me and placed the blade of a knife to my throat. I felt a sharp pain as he pressed the tip to my neck.

"Tell her or she dies!"

He meant it. He intended to kill me. Avan held out a hand, reaching for me.

"No! I'm the one you want! Don't bring her into this, please!"

The blade pushed against the pulse in my neck.

"Tell her now! Tell her what you did to my son!"

Tears streamed down Avan's cheeks. His fingers gripped the side of the tub. "I killed him!"

Kaine's grip on me loosened, and I spoke before the knife moved from my throat.

"What?"

Avan's eyes flicked to his hand gripping the tub, then back to me. I was aware that Kaine had stepped away from me. No doubt he was standing in the doorway, hoping for an argument to ensue, waiting for a show. I'd disappoint him and pitched my voice low.

"You're lying. You wouldn't do that."

My chest was on fire. His eyes flicked back to me and he said it again.

"I killed him."

I shook my head. "No, you didn't. You wouldn't have."

"I wish I hadn't." He paused, sniffing, wiping away a tear from his cheek. "But I did." He looked away from me, broken and sad.

I didn't say anything. I couldn't say anything. I stood there with my hands on either side of my head, pulling at my hair, not remembering how they got there.

"Two fucking years, Avan," I snapped. "How could you keep this from me?"

"I'm sorry," he said, voice hushed. "I've tried to tell you so many times, but you kept-"

"It's my fault?"

"No, I'm not saying that!"

I didn't want to hear more. I stormed off, pushing past Kaine and falling onto the bed. I buried my face into the mattress. My mother had told me that Avan and I were moving too fast with our relationship. She warned me I'd get hurt. I'd laughed her off, but she'd been right. How stupid I'd been!

I heard Kaine walk out, heard his heavy metal-toed boots stomp up the stairs. The door locked with a click.

Avan's voice called out to me, his pain echoing off the walls of the bathroom. "I'm sorry!"

Exhaustion washed over me in waves. It overtook me, overwhelming my senses and thoughts, promising escape. Despite there being no covers on the bed, despite my anger at Avan, I drifted away.

"AVAN, LET HIM GO!"

Avan held a vise grip around the boy's throat. I shoved my way through the screaming crowd.

"Avan, that's enough!"

The boy was gasping, kicking, struggling for air. I pressed my face against the cage.

"You're killing him, stop!"

I AWOKE WITH A START, my hair pasted to the side of my face. It was so real, I could still hear the crowd, smell the beer, feel the fright from Avan's opponent. But it faded, and

I realized we were still in the basement. I wasn't watching the death of that boy.

I fell back onto the bed with a groan. I raised my arm to cover my eyes, an automatic gesture despite the darkness. I thought about the dream, the nightmare. I thought about the boy, thought about Avan. I had never seen him lose control in the cage. I hadn't seen him do so much as celebrate a victory without helping his opponents to their feet, hugging them, congratulating them. The remorseless, cold, unfeeling monster in my dream wasn't my Avan.

The boy's death had been an accident.

I took a deep breath and made my way quietly into the bathroom. I sat on the edge of the tub.

"How did it happen?"

Chapter Twenty-Five

Avan opened his eyes and looked at me.

"What happened, Avan?"

He grimaced and sat up, lowering his eyes. "Do you remember the day we met?"

It came back so vividly that for a moment I was out of this basement and back at the coffee shop.

I'd been on my way out, a steaming cup in my hands, just as Avan was on his way in. When I slipped on a patch of ice coating the stairs, I was caught by a pair of warm and muscular arms before I hit the ground. His smile, crooked and bright, was the first thing I saw. His eyes, welcoming and warm, were the second.

I was mortified when I saw I'd spilled my coffee all over his jacket. Mercifully, he paid it no mind and offered to buy me another cup. Charmed by his kindness, I accepted and sat with him inside instead of leaving right away. Avan got whipped cream on the end of his nose, and the ice was broken. We laughed and talked and sipped our mugs until the early afternoon sky grew pink.

I smiled at the memory, warmed by its closeness.

"You practically swept me off my feet," I said.

He smiled a small smile, a forced smile. It faded as he went on. "Do you remember what I told you?"

I knew by his voice it was bad. I wanted to talk about it. I didn't want to talk about it. I changed the subject.

"You told me how to pronounce your name. Gavin without the G."

He shook his head. He was growing impatient. "About growing up in Foster Care."

I couldn't. No matter how hard I tried, my brain fogged. I only remembered the scars. I could see them now, the dark dots on his fingers and the back of his hands. Against his now pale skin, they screamed at me. They begged me to look at them. I looked away as I answered him.

"You said it was Hell."

He stayed silent for several long moments before continuing.

"I was the brown kid who was always in trouble. They'd hit me with belts, power cords, coat hangers, whatever they could find. That's how it was for a long time. There were some nice homes, but no one wanted me. I'd be moved the moment I'd start to feel safe. Most of the homes they put me in were abusive, and I was-"

He paused. His voice became rougher, though the softness was still there.

"I was nothing but a punching bag."

I reached out to touch him and he recoiled, pressing a hand to his mouth. He looked away from me.

"Things got better after the Gutierrezes took me in, but the damage was done. I had everything I wanted and I still felt like a piece of shit."

I wanted to touch him, to kiss him, to comfort him, but I didn't move. It wasn't right to interfere in his story.

"I was never enough. When I discovered mixed martial arts, I- everything changed. I was finally good at something, finally worth something, ya know?"

He paused, his eyes flitting to the tiled wall beside him, and he was gone again, reliving a memory, watching a fight that I couldn't see. Again, he'd effortlessly managed to shut me out. I wanted to be angry with him, but the hurt in his voice and the downward curve of his lips kept my anger in check. His hand rose to his mouth. He kept it there, his words barely a whisper, his eyes shining.

"I see him every time I close my eyes."

I knew who he was talking about. He was talking about Kaine's son. Immediately, my mind flashed to the nightmares I witnessed for so many years. I'd wake up to find Avan panting and sweating, his hands gripping the bed sheets. Now I knew. I knew the exact moment that visited each night.

"Kole was my friend." Avan continued. "We went to fight camp together. We trained together. That night? I cared more about winning that damn fight than I cared about him. I should've seen the signs. I should've seen that he was struggling, but I-"

He stopped. He clasped a hand over his mouth as if his next words were acidic.

"I kept hitting him, for three whole rounds. I just kept hitting him and hitting him. When I went for the final kick-"

He paused again, tearful.

"I kicked him, and he fell and he started seizing and-"

He stopped again, unable to go on. My next question came without thought.

"Who burned you?"

He ran a thumb over a burn scar, blinking thoughtfully. "I did."

It didn't take long for me to understand. Some of those scars were no more than a year old. God, how long had he done this to himself?

How had I not noticed his pain?

His guilt?

His trauma?

Realization pricked me. Nerves tore through my stomach in a painful surge of nausea.

Stupid, stupid me!

I'd chosen not to see it because I didn't want to. I'd chosen not to hear it whenever he brought it up.

It was all right in front of me now, the facts I chose to ignore. That's when it hit me. Avan's guilt drove him to fight, to be willingly lashed in my place, to obey Kaine's every command. I felt a warm surge of empathy towards him. I knew what the burden of guilt carried, the tremendous weight it placed onto one's shoulders.

Didn't I feel the same guilt after finding my brother?

"Avan," I said, very softly, and waited.

Finally, he looked at me, expression pained, and I remembered contemplating killing Kaine with his gun. The thought of it was enough to make my stomach clench. Even though he tortured Avan, even though he ripped our lives from us, I couldn't imagine living with the guilt of taking his life.

With clarity, I remembered finding a stack of papers on Avan's desk: a liability waiver. My eyes locked on the bold print immediately.

MMA is a very dangerous sport. You could get seriously injured or killed.

With regret, I'd backed away, startled when I saw Avan's name scribbled on the dotted line in his messy backward handwriting.

He'd known what he was getting himself into. He'd known the risks, the consequences. Yet he signed the waiver anyway, just like Kole must've done.

"I'm a killer," Avan said, suddenly. "I'm the reason he's dead. I'm the reason we're here. I'm the reason Kaine-"

"Stop it!" I banged my fist on the side of the tub. I couldn't hear anymore, didn't want to hear anymore. I needed it to stop. The moment I saw Avan flinch for the second time, I knew I couldn't let my anger overtake me. I softened my voice and took his fingers in my own.

"Stop it. This isn't your fault. None of it was your fault. There were doctors there, Avan. It was their job to watch that boy, not yours. He knew what he was getting into, like you did. It wasn't your fault. You hear me?"

He looked at me, and I saw he heard but didn't believe. I knew he wouldn't. It would take years for him to believe me, no matter how many times I pointed out the truth. I couldn't save him unless he was willing to see it. He had to be ready to forgive himself first.

I didn't say anything more. It wouldn't help him even if I had. I climbed into the bathtub and lay down beside him.

"Sleep, Avan," I whispered, closing my eyes.

"I-"

"Shh," I said, my eyes still closed. "Stop. Please. No more. Lay with me and sleep."

I heard the blanket ruffle as he settled beside me. I felt his fingers on my chin as he tried to soothe me. I smelled the stench of his breath as he whispered, "I'm sorry."

THE BASEMENT STAIRS creaked as I walked down. I knew what I'd find: a boy hanging from a support beam. But my legs didn't protest. My pace didn't slow. When I saw the lifeless face, my blood ran cold. This wasn't my brother.

It was Avan!

I AWOKE WITH A SHARP cry. Avan shot up, grimacing, and stared at me, his brow furrowed with concern. He touched my arm, fingertips slick against my clammy skin. His eyes darted this way and that, looking for the threat. When he saw that Kaine wasn't around, he looked at me again, smoothing my hair.

"What happened?" he asked, voice hushed. "Are you okay?"

Part of me was aware that he was here with me, but my subconscious mind flashed to his dream face, lifeless and blue, in the place of my brother. I couldn't shake the image. My body was burning, and I grimaced when Avan went to hold me. He jerked away from me, apologizing, his expression horrified.

Now you know how I feel.

"I'm okay," I assured him, despite the burning.

Now I knew how he felt, finally understood why he was always so quick to reassure me, to comfort me, to gloss over his suffering.

We sat in an uneasy silence for a long moment.

"You're not the only one keeping secrets," I said, suddenly, my heart hammering. "There's something I've been hiding from you, too."

Avan's eyebrows rose ever so slightly, but he didn't say anything, so I continued.

"I told you that my brother committed suicide, but I never told you why."

"You don't need to-"

"Yes, I do, Avan!"

He flinched for a second time. Avan, who wasn't afraid of anything, had flinched because of *me*.

I wondered, and then I knew. It was Kaine who broke Avan. Kaine who lashed Avan into submission. Kaine who stripped away Avan's will to live. I hated him for it.

I took a breath. I needed to say this.

"It was the concussions from football. He started hearing voices and seeing things that weren't there. No doctors would help him. I don't know, but he couldn't take it anymore and he-" I stopped. Memories flickered through my head. I shook them off and started again.

"That's why I worry so much, Avan. Seeing you get hit like you do. It takes me back to Gabe, to what he did."

I risked a glance at Avan. He wanted to hold me. I could see it, but he restrained himself.

"I'm not scared of you getting hurt. Not now that I've seen you like-" I swallowed. He knew what I was thinking. He had to have known. I went on, slower. "I'm scared of losing you, Avan. I'm scared of you getting hit so hard that you'll suffer like Gabe suffered. I don't... I don't want to find you dead, too."

I was crying now. I didn't tell him about the nightmare, and as soon as I saw his eyes shine, I knew I never would. He touched my face with trembling fingers and brushed away my tears.

"You'll never have to worry again."

He said it so calmly, so matter-of-factly, that for the first time in weeks, I thought we would make it out.

NO ONE CAME BACK INTO the basement after that. Not even Kaine. I lost track of the days, the weeks, the months. Avan and I lay in the tub, sick, injured, weak. We soiled ourselves, too malnourished to get up to go to the toilet. We developed lingering coughs. Our chests hurt with every breath.

Avan was fading, drifting in and out the way he had when we first arrived, though he hadn't been drugged.

"What do you love about me?" I asked.

Avan's lowered eyes rose slowly to meet mine. His brow creased.

"What?"

I repeated my question. He seemed lost, like he was trying to put the question together in his mind. He lowered his eyes again.

"You help me forget." He paused, deep in his thoughts. "You help me forget what happened. You help me forget what I did. The way you look at me, you see me as someone who's-someone who's perfect. I was broken before I met you. Now I'm whole. You make me whole."

I wanted to tell him everything. I wanted to let him know how I felt about him, how he had made me whole by simply being in my life, how he became a part of me as I had become a part of him.

I was distracted the moment I took Avan's hand. The tips of his fingers were cold, and, as the minutes dragged on, his hands followed, then his wrists, and his arms. I ran my hands over him, praying that friction would save him. But he stayed cold. Avan was always warm to the touch. He was like his own sun. Now, that sun, my sun, was dying.

Chapter Twenty-Six

The basement door slammed open. Avan was dragged out of the bathtub and beaten on the floor. Avan was forced from the bathtub, out of my arms. The men kicked him from all sides until he curled into a ball.

I climbed from the bathtub, falling and catching myself with my hands. I shook from weakness, from hunger, from desperation. The men saw and grabbed me. They dragged me to the same support beam that Avan was tied to nearly a month ago and secured my wrists. I fought uselessly against them, my starved body losing energy quickly, my weak muscles straining with what little strength I still had, as Kaine kicked Avan again and again.

"Backing out of your last fight?" Kaine taunted, circling Avan. "I knew you were a coward."

Avan struggled to crawl away. Kaine went for another kick to Avan's side, and Avan collapsed.

"Only a coward would kill a boy," Kaine panted. "That's what you did, and that's who you are."

Avan rolled on his back, coughing and wheezing. Kaine walked in a tight circle around him.

"You're not a fighter. You're pathetic. You're weak!"

Kaine motioned to the men. They grabbed Avan by the arms and forced him up.

"You killed him!" Kaine snapped.

The men tied Avan's wrists to the wooden beam across from me. They forced him to stand, loosening the rope so his toes touched the ground. Avan's face twisted as he shifted his weight, seeking comfort which eluded him. The movement caused fresh blood to stain the cloth around his feet and pulled an agonized sound from him. Kaine smiled.

"She finally knows what you did, Gutierrez." He stared at me, and I shot him a dark glare. He ignored me, pulling out his gun and pistol whipping Avan. Avan coughed and lowered his head, hiding his face from Kaine, hiding his pain from me. I whimpered.

Hit me, Kaine... Hit me!

Kaine frowned, placing the gun on a nearby table. When he spoke again, his voice was low, menacing.

"She finally knows what worthless scum you are."

Avan mumbled, voice quiet, words unintelligible. Kaine grabbed Avan's hair, jerking his head up. Avan winced. Blood gushed from his broken nose.

"What was that?"

Avan's eyes flicked to Kaine. He didn't look like him anymore. He whispered the words, "I'm sorry."

Kaine let go of Avan's hair. Avan's head fell forward. One of the other men walked up to us holding a bamboo cane in his hands. Kaine took it, bending it and testing its flexibility.

No!

"Kaine, wait!" I yelled.

He paused behind Avan. I took a deep breath, my entire upper body burning from the action.

"I know how you feel. I lost my brother. It hurts like Hell, I know, but killing Avan won't bring your son back."

Kaine held the cane tighter. My words weren't helping. They weren't making him understand that what he was doing, what he'd been doing, was wrong. I jerked and twisted with the last of my vitality. After giving up, I looked at Avan and saw he wasn't trying to support himself anymore. He'd gone completely limp. His blood dripped onto the floor.

"I'm sorry," he said again.

Kaine stepped back.

"You're too late."

It was useless. It was always useless. Everything we'd done, everything we'd fought for, was all a waste. We were going to die. And Avan would be the first to go.

Kaine swung the weapon, striking Avan across the back. The thuds rang out, loud and sickening as Kaine continued, lashing Avan from his shoulders to his calves.

"Kill me!" I cried.

At my cry, Avan lifted his head. The action was slow, heavy, like it took the last of his strength. A stream of red dripped into his mouth, down his chin, and stained his already bloody shorts. Kaine kept hitting Avan with all his might. Avan didn't react. The only indication that Kaine was still whipping him were the thuds and twitches of his body at every blow. He wasn't wincing, just standing there, his eyes empty, his mouth agape, watching me without a hint of recognition.

I was losing him with every stroke of the cane.

He didn't acknowledge me. He didn't even blink. His mind was somewhere far away, escaping the reality of his shattered body. His chest fluttered, his lungs barely taking in the air he needed to survive. His pupils dilated. His lips were turning blue.

I shuddered. This wasn't Avan anymore. This was a wounded animal, using every last ounce of its will to stay alive. Seeing him like this, so broken he seemed to welcome the torture, was worse than seeing him writhe in unbearable agony. He bowed his head once more, and though I knew he was still breathing, it felt like he was already gone.

Kaine stopped. Someone was banging on the door upstairs. "Watch them." He dropped the cane on the floor.

The three men surrounded us as Kaine made his way upstairs, as if we could attempt an escape. There was muffled talk, then the talk became louder. I didn't catch the words, but there was yelling and footsteps coming down the hall above us. There were others in the house!

I opened my mouth to scream, to shout, to yell for help, please, God, help us!

One of the guards picked up the gun and hit me across the face.

My vision blurred and ringing filled my ears. Everything was getting dark. I was looking through a tunnel at Avan, his blurry silhouette hanging, unmoving.

Avan

There were others in the room. I felt them, felt the warmth of their bodies.

Avan

Muffled voices. Rapid movement behind and beside me. The absence of the men. But my focus was on him.

Avan

Someone loosened my bonds. I fell into a man's arms. His scent was too clean, not at all like the musky scent of Kaine and the men. He was speaking to me, asking me questions, but my focus was elsewhere, my eyes not leaving the dark blurry figure that was Avan. I was laid on the floor. The man in black was talking frantically. The figure in black untied Avan's wrists. Metal things glinted from his belt.

Avan fell into the man's arms, unresponsive. He was laid on the ground beside me as if he was as fragile as a butterfly. I saw the man touch something on his shoulder. His voice trailed off as my thoughts spun and whirled, my focus fading slowly with his muffled words. Avan was the last thing I saw. He wasn't breathing. He was still, pale, silent, dying.

Avan

Chapter Twenty-Seven

"What happened? Where was she? How did you find her?"

A voice, female, anxious, distant, found my ears. Another voice, male, spoke softly back to her. I only caught snippets of his words.

"Wasn't paying the rent ... Saw them in the basement ... nearly dead ... lucky to be alive... suspects ran ..."

"They?" questioned the female, sounding surprised.

"Yes," the male said. "Your daughter wasn't the only one there."

There was a long silence, then the female, who I finally recognized as my mother, spoke again.

"Did he have black hair? Green eyes?"

Avan... They were talking about Avan!

"I'm afraid I can't discuss that with you, ma'am. Let us know when she wakes up. We've got a few questions to ask her."

His footsteps, long and light, faded with my consciousness.

Time came and went. For the briefest of moments, I was aware of people standing over me with needles and charts. Then, I was aware of nothing.

Day 1

MY VISION WAS BLURRY. Every movement was painful. Through the cloudiness, my eyes took in the sight of a woman dozing in a chair.

"Mom?"

The woman's eyes snapped open. Her head shot up and she slid from the chair.

"Oh my God," she said, driven to tears. "Oh, sweetie!"

She held me gently, but I didn't want her or her concern. I wanted Avan.

"Where is he?"

She looked at me, confused. She raised an eyebrow.

"Where's Avan?" I clarified.

Her face became soft. She stroked my hair.

"They're doing what they can, hun."

Two years. Two years of radio silence and this is how she acted, like she suddenly cared? My voice was flat, emotionless.

"Really? You think you can be motherly now, like flipping a switch, after what you've done for two years?" I shook my head. I hadn't even tried to hide the snarkiness in my voice. "I want to see him."

"You can't see him right now, sweetheart."

My eyebrows drew down over my eyes. My mouth set in a hard line.

"Why not?"

Mom didn't answer. She looked over her shoulder at the police officers who'd come through the opened door. I knew why they were here, but I didn't want to talk to them. I just wanted to see Avan.

"They didn't touch me," was all I said when they asked about sexual assault.

"Are you sure, honey?"

I could feel my mother looking at me. I snapped at her.

"Why wouldn't I be sure?"

"You may not remember. They could've drugged you and then-"

"They didn't touch me!" My mother started in her chair. She wasn't used to me raising my voice. "They didn't touch me. Avan made sure of it."

"Avan?"

"Yes, Mom."

She didn't say anything more. She looked away.

"I know you don't like him, Mom. I know you're afraid that he'll hurt me because he's damaged or whatever. I'm alive because of him. I'm happy because of him. If you were ever around, you would know that. I haven't been this happy since Gabe-"

My mother waved her hand. Her eyes were wet. I stopped talking. I was hitting a raw spot by mentioning Gabe, her only son, her firstborn, her favorite. She swallowed, and I felt guilty. I wished she hadn't come.

"Please," I begged. "I need to see him."

My heart rate rose. My chest burned.

"Who do you need to see, dear?" asked the nurse, but before I could answer, my mother said, "He's a patient here."

"What's his name?"

I was ready. "Avan Gutierrez."

"Are you family?"

"He's my husband." I said, daring my mother to contradict me.

I could see my mother scowling at me from the corner of my eye. The nurse's eyes glistened.

The nurse nodded at me. "Not yet. We have a trauma team working on your husband. You can see him as soon as he's stable."

I shook my head. "I need to see him now."

"Sweetie," my mother said, placing a hand on my arm. "You should stay in bed and rest."

"No, Mom!" I snapped. My head throbbed. My wounds throbbed. My heart throbbed. I needed to see him. And nothing was going to stop me.

Day 4

DRAGGING MY IV STAND beside me, I followed the doctor to Avan's room. For three whole days, I begged to see him, ignoring my mother's demands and the nurses' recommendations. Finally, they gave in.

All three of them walked with me, the doctor included. I moved as fast as my body allowed, pushing through pain, my trembling muscles, and the irritating friction of my robber-soled socks against the smooth tile. I watched the lights reflecting off the floor as I walked, not needing to look ahead of me. My mother held me by one arm, the nurse by the other, and the doctor led the way. I watched each light disappear beneath my feet and wished our trauma could disappear that easily. I knew it wouldn't. It would be years and millions of steps forward before we would be free of this nightmare.

The doctor halted. He paused, his hand on the handle of the door. It felt like everything was happening in slow motion. All I wanted to do was push past him, open the door, and cling to Avan's bedside. But I didn't. I stood and waited staring at my feet. The doctor's voice was coated with sympathy, and something else that made my heart sink - uncertainty.

"We had to put him into a medically induced coma so that he could heal. He's on a ventilator, but don't be concerned. It helps him breathe."

I nodded slowly, a chill rushing through my veins, anxiety pricking me. I didn't know what I'd see or how I'd react. The images floating through my imagination were far more frightening than the image the doctor provided.

The doctor opened the door and stepped out of the way.

Avan's parents weren't there. That was the first thing I noticed. The second thing was the whisper of the ventilator, the soft movement of air flowing in and out of Avan's lungs. I heard the fading footsteps of the doctor and the nurse speaking quietly to my mother in the hallway, but my focus was on the tube in Avan's throat, the bandages around his feet, and the machines that kept him alive.

I eased myself in the chair beside the bed. His leg was propped up, his knee in a brace. His head wasn't set forward as I had expected. It was tilted to the side, as if he were simply taking a power nap before being discharged from the hospital. I took his fingers in my own. Kissing his knuckles, I whispered through my tears.

"Stay alive for me."

Avan's heart gave out that night.

I'd barely fallen asleep on the small recliner in a corner of the room when one of his monitors screamed. The sound woke me instantly. Fight or flight took control, but instead of fleeing or fighting, I froze. I stared helplessly at the straight line on his heart monitor, wanting to do something, but unable to. It reminded me so much of Avan's whipping, of his beating, of every time I'd simply watched his torture, that I screamed. Nurses and doctors rushed in with a cart and clustered around him. One guided me out of the room.

"What's happening?" My voice was an ugly mix of panic, anger, and fear. "What's wrong with him?"

No longer as gentle, she pushed me out of the room with a greater sense of urgency and closed the door behind us. I broke away from her grasp and reached towards the small window of the door, my chest and stomach burning. I looked through it and immediately wished I hadn't.

Day 7

...

Day 10

I DIDN'T LEAVE AVAN'S side. I sat in the chair beside his bed, napped on the small couch in the corner, and tried to imagine him awake. He was finally strong enough to breathe on his own, the nurse removing his chest tube earlier that morning. All I had to do now was wait.

My mother had gone downstairs to the hospital cafeteria. I'd eaten liquids and soft foods that were easy to digest, steaming broth and gelatin and pudding. As I sat back, wondering how Avan would react to the food, I caught faint movement.

"Avan?"

I moved from the couch to the recliner, sitting down and taking Avan by the hand. His fingers twitched against my palm. Then, very slowly, his eyes fluttered open.

"Grace..."

He trailed off, his words fading into mumbles. I shushed him gently, squeezing his fingers, and fighting to restrain myself from hugging him.

"I'm here, Avan."

His eyes held me. His voice was scratchy, his words nearly inaudible. "Are you..."

His voice, raspy and low, faded away again. His eyes squeezed shut as he tried to move.

Oh, Avan. My sweet selfless thoughtful Avan.

"Yes," I soothed, running my fingers through his hair. "Yes, sweetheart. I'm okay."

His oxygen mask fogged as he sighed, closing his eyes. For a moment, I thought about calling a nurse, but then his eyes opened. His next words came out in a single breath.

"All of this is my fault."

I wanted to snap at him, to force those thoughts out of his head. I shushed him again, caressing the side of his face with my fingers instead. His expression, immeasurably sad, pierced me. I pressed his knuckles to my lips.

"Don't think like that," I said, my words muffled by his fingers. "You can't think like that."

His eyes flicked up, watching something above me. When his fingers tensed, I looked behind me. I saw the television hung in the upper corner of the room. A flood of emotions welled up at the sight of Kaine's mugshot: anger, hatred, and the strongest of all, guilt.

I pushed them down and returned my focus to Avan, whose heart rate had spiked. In his eyes, I saw clearly that he was remembering everything, reliving all of the hell we'd endured. I stood and laid my palms on either side of his face, my fingers running over his hot skin.

"It's okay, Avan. Look at me. It's okay. Just breathe. I'm right here."

His hands found my elbows as he inhaled a few ragged breaths. I breathed with him. He closed his eyes, his heart rate slowing.

"That's it. Just keep breathing."

For a moment, our lungs, our chests, our hearts, moved as one. When his heart rate became normal again, I leaned in close, resting my forehead against his, and closed my eyes.

"You don't have to carry this weight alone, Avan. I'm right here with you. And I'll be there for you every step of the way."

His body shuddered and I pulled back, my fingers still on his cheeks. With a weak hand, he reached up and pulled down the oxygen mask.

"I'm sorry, Grace."

His words were clearer now, his pain more audible. I kissed his hair, his temple, the side of his nose, my lips careful against his battered body. I ran a hand over his hair then took him in my arms as gently as I could.

"It's over, Avan," I whispered. "It's all over. I've got you."

He wrapped his arms around me, fingers gripping the sleeves of my hospital gown.

"I'm sorry," he said again. "I'm sorry."

He repeated himself over and over, punctuated by one broken sob after another. A hot, bitter lump rose in my throat. My eyes welled painfully. No, I couldn't cry now. Not now. I gulped it down and closed my eyes.

"Shh," I soothed. "He can't hurt you anymore. You're safe. I've got you. You're safe now."

He sobbed harder, realizing the truth of my words, the hell we'd been through was hitting him all at once. I cradled the back of his head as he'd done for me so many times before, and drew him closer, holding him as tight as I dared.

And nothing in the world could've encouraged me to let go.

Epilogue

The heat of my laptop was comforting, as were my flannel pajamas and the dimly lit apartment. A gentle spring rain had begun to fall, and out of boredom, I searched for homes for sale. Oh, we were happy in the apartment, but there were moments it felt like our home was tying us to the past, a past we wanted to leave behind.

I scrolled through them, loving the freedom and openness they represented, the freedom Avan and I once took for granted. Not anymore. One particular house caught my eye. Its tall windows, reflecting a portrait of the woods, nearly took up the entire front of the house. They seemed familiar, though my mind couldn't pinpoint where I'd seen them before. When I clicked on the next photo, my breathing sped and my heart raced. It was a photo of the inside, light spilling through the wall of windows onto the rustic walls and plaid furniture.

I knew this house.

"Hey."

I looked up, my heart rate slowing. Avan stood in the doorway, his dark curls made even darker and curlier from a shower. He looked relaxed in his baggy t-shirt and boxer shorts. The scars on his knee were fading.

He smirked shyly, his voice playful. "Race ya to bed."

Not much of a race, considering his crutches and knee brace, but a cute gesture.

My Avan, forever knowing just what to say.

I smiled at him, closed the laptop, and followed him into our bedroom. Avan was my future, not that house.